Finger Posts On The Way Of Life

By
T. S. Arthur

SHADOWS FROM A CLOUDED BROW.

A LITTLE thing clouded the brow of Mrs. Abercrombie—a very little thing. But if she had known how wide the shadows were often diffused, and how darkly they fell, at times, on some hearts, she would have striven more earnestly, we may believe, to keep the sky of her spirit undimmed.

It will not be uninstructive to note the incidents, in a single day, of Mrs. Abercrombie's life—to mark the early cloud upon her brow, and then to glance at the darkly falling shadows.

Mr. Abercrombie was a man of sensitive feelings, and though he had striven for many years to overcome his sensitiveness, he had been no more able to change this hereditary weakness than the leopard his spots or the Ethiopian his skin. At home, the lightest jar of discord disturbed him painfully, and the low vibration ceased not, often, for many hours. The clouded brow of his wife ever threw his heart into shadow; and the dusky vail was never removed, until sunlight radiated again from her countenance. It was all in vain that he tried to be indifferent to these changeful moods—to keep his spirits above their influence: in the very effort at disenthralment he was more firmly bound.

From some cause, unknown to her husband, there was a cloud on the brow of Mrs. Abercrombie one morning, as she took her place at the breakfast-table. Mr. Abercrombie was reading, with his usual interest, the newspaper, and the children were sporting in the nursery, when the bell summoned them to the dining-room. All gathered, with pleasant thoughts of good cheer, around the table, and Mr. Abercrombie, after helping the little ones, was about mentioning to his wife some pleasant piece of news which he had just been reading, when, on lifting his eyes to her countenance, he saw that it was clouded. The words died on his lips; a shadow darkened over his feelings, and the meal passed in almost total silence—at least so far as he was concerned. Once or twice he ventured a remark to Mrs. Abercrombie; but the half-fretful tone in which she replied, only disturbed him the more.

Soon the pleasant aspect of the children's countenances changed, and they became captious and irritable. Both parents were fretted at this reaction upon their own states of mind, and manifested, at some slight misconduct on the part of one or two of the children, a degree of ill-nature that instantly transferred itself to those against whom it was directed, and became apparent in their intercourse one with another.

Before summoned from the nursery, these children were playing together in the utmost harmony and good feeling; on returning thereto, the activity of another and far less amiable spirit was manifest; and instead of merry shouts and joyous laughter, angry words and complaining cries sounded through the apartment.

As Mr. Abercrombie left the house, Mrs. Abercrombie entered the nursery, attracted by the notes of discord. Had there been sunshine on her countenance, and firm but gentle remonstrance on her tongue, a quick change would have become apparent. But, ere this, the shadows she had thrown around her had darkened the atmosphere of her dwelling, and were now reflected back upon her heart, enshrouding it in deeper gloom. The want of harmony among her children increased her mental disturbance, obscured her perceptions, and added to her state of irritability. She could not speak calmly to them, nor wisely endeavour to restore the harmony which had been lost. Her words, therefore, while, by their authoritative force, they subdued the storm, left the sky black with clouds that poured down another and fiercer tempest the moment her presence was removed.

But this state of things could not be permitted. The mother reappeared, and, after some hurried inquiries into the cause of disturbance among her children, took for granted the statement of those who were most forward in excusing themselves and accusing others, and unwisely resorted to punishment— unwisely, in the first place, because she decided hastily and from first appearances; and in the second place, because she was in no state of mind to administer punishment. The consequence was, that she punished those least to blame, and thereby did a great wrong. Of this she was made fully aware after it was too late. Then, indignant at the false accusation by which she had been led into the commission of an unjust act, she visited her wrath with undue severity, and in unseemly passion, upon the heads of the real offenders.

By this time the children were in a state of intimidation. It was plain that their mother was fairly aroused, and each deemed it best to be as quiet and inoffensive as possible. The reappearance of harmony being thus restored, Mrs. Abercrombie, whose head and heart were now both throbbing with pain, retired in a most unhappy state of mind to her chamber, where she threw herself into a large chair, feeling unutterably wretched.

And what was the origin of all this discord and misery? Why came that cloud, in the beginning, to the brow of Mrs. Abercrombie—that cloud, whose shadow had already exercised so baleful an influence? The cause was slight, very slight. But do not, fair reader, blame Mrs. Abercrombie too severely, nor say this cause was censurably inadequate. The touch of a feather will hurt an inflamed part. Ah! does not your own experience in life affirm this. Think of the last time the cloud was on your brow, and ask yourself as to the adequacy of the cause.

"But what was the cause?" you inquire. Well, don't smile: a pair of gaiters had been sent home for Mrs. Abercrombie, late on the evening previous, and one of her first acts in the morning was to try them on. They did not fit! Now, Mrs. Abercrombie intended to go out on that very morning, and she wished to wear these gaiters. "Enough to fret her, I should say!" exclaims one fair reader. "A slight cause, indeed!" says another, tossing her curls; "men are great philosophers!"

We crave pardon, gentle ladies all, if, in our estimate of causes, we have spoken too lightly of this. But we have, at least, stated the case fairly. Mrs. Abercrombie's brow was clouded because the new gaiters did not fit her handsome foot—a member, by the way, of which she was more than a little vain.

For an hour Mrs. Abercrombie remained alone in her chamber, feeling very sad; for, in that time, reflection had come, and she was by no means satisfied with the part she had been playing, nor altogether unconscious of the fact that from her clouded brow had fallen the shadows now darkening over her household. As soon as she had gained sufficient control of herself to act toward her children more wisely and affectionately, the mother took her place in the nursery, and with a tenderness of manner that acted like a charm, attracted her little ones to her side, and inspired them with a new and better spirit. To them sunshine was restored again; and the few rays that penetrated to the mother's heart, lighted its dim chambers, and touched it with a generous warmth.

But the shadows from Mrs. Abercrombie's clouded brow fell not alone upon her household. The spirit that pervades the home-circle is often carried forth by those who go out into the world. It was so in this case. Mr. Abercrombie's feelings were overcast with shadows when he entered the store. There was a pressure, in consequence, upon his bosom, and a state of irritability which he essayed, though feebly and ineffectually, to overcome.

"Where is Edward?" he inquired, soon after his arrival.

Edward was a lad, the son of a poor widow, who had recently been employed in Mr. Abercrombie's store.

"He hasn't come yet," was answered.

"Not come yet?" said Mr. Abercrombie, in a fretful tone.

"No, sir."

"This is the third time he has been late within the past week, is it not?"

"Yes, sir."

"Very well: it shall be the last time."

At this moment the boy came in. Mr. Abercrombie looked at him sternly for a moment, and then said—

"You won't suit me, sir. I took you on trial, and am satisfied. You can go home."

The poor lad's face crimsoned instantly, and he tried to say something about his mother's being sick, but Mr. Abercrombie waved his hand impatiently, and told him that he didn't wish to hear any excuse.

Scarcely had the boy left the presence of Mr. Abercrombie, ere this hasty action was repented of. But the merchant's pride of consistency was strong: he was not the man to acknowledge an error. His word had passed, and could not be recalled. Deeper were the shadows that now fell upon his heart—more fretted the state of mind that supervened.

Ah! the shadows would have been deeper still, could he have seen that unhappy boy a little while afterward, as, with his face buried in the pillow that supported the head of his sick mother, he sobbed until his whole frame quivered. Had Mr. Abercrombie only asked the reason why his appearance at the store was so late on this morning, he would have learned that the delay had been solely occasioned by needful attendance on his sick and almost helpless mother; and on a little further inquiry, humanity would have dictated approval rather than censure and punishment. But, touching all this painful consequence of his ill-nature, the merchant knew nothing. How rarely do we become cognizant of the evil wrought upon others by our hasty and ill-judged actions!

The shadow was still on Mr. Abercrombie's feelings, when, half an hour afterward, a man came to him and said—

"It will be impossible for me to lift the whole of that note to-day."

"You'll have to do it," was the quiet answer. Mr. Abercrombie frowned darkly as he thus replied.

"Don't say that, Mr. Abercrombie. I only want help to the amount of two hundred dollars."

"I do say it. You must raise the money somewhere else. I don't like this way of doing business. When a man gives his note, he should make it a point of honour to pay it."

"Oh, very well," said the man. "I'm sorry if I've troubled you. I'll get the money from a friend. Good morning."

And he turned off abruptly, and left the store. Mr. Abercrombie felt rebuked. He had a large balance in the bank, and could have accommodated him without the smallest inconvenience. In another state of mind he would have done so cheerfully.

"O dear!" sighed the unhappy merchant, speaking mentally; "what has come over me? I'm losing all control of myself. This will never, never do. I must set a guard upon my lips."

And he did so. Conscious of his state of irritability, he subdued his tones of voice, and restrained utterance when tempted to angry or inconsiderate speech. Not again during the day was he guilty of such inexcusable conduct as in the instances mentioned; yet the shadow remained upon his feelings, strive as he would to throw off the gloomy impression.

It was late in the day when Mr. Abercrombie turned his steps homeward. How little was he satisfied with himself! And now, when he remembered, with painful distinctness, the clouded brow of his wife, how little promise was there of home-sunlight, to dispel the gloom of his own feelings!

As the hand of the merchant rested upon his own door, he almost dreaded to enter. He shrank from meeting that clouded visage. The shadows were dark when he left in the morning, and experience told him that he need scarcely hope to find them dispelled. Happily, though still in the sky, the clouds were broken, and gleams of sunshine came breaking through. Ah! if they had only possessed sufficient power to disperse the shadows that all day long had been gathering around the heart of Mr. Abercrombie! But that was impossible. Self-respect had been forfeited; and a consciousness of having, in his impatient haste, acted unjustly, haunted his thoughts. And so, the shadows that were not to be dispersed by the feeble sun-rays from the countenance of his wife, gradually diffused themselves, until the light that struggled with them grew pale.

"Did you know," said Mrs. Abercrombie, breaking in upon the oppressive silence that succeeded, after all had retired for the night but herself and husband, "that the mother of Edward Wilson is very poor and in a decline?"

"I was not aware of it," was the brief response.

"It is so. Mrs. Archer was here this afternoon, and was telling me about them. Mrs. Wilson, who, until within a few weeks past, has been able to earn something, is now so weak that she cannot leave her bed, and is solely dependent on the earnings of her son. How much do you pay him?"

"Only three dollars a week," answered Mr. Abercrombie, shading his face with his hand.

"Only three dollars! How can they live on that? Mrs. Archer says that Edward is one of the best of lads—that he nurses his mother, and cares for her with unfailing tenderness; indeed, he is her only attendant. They are too poor to pay for the services of a domestic. Could you not afford to increase his wages?"

"I might, perhaps," said Mr. Abercrombie, abstractedly, still shading his face.

"I wish you could," was the earnest reply. "It will be a real charity."

Mr. Abercrombie made no response; and his wife pursued the subject no further. But the former lay awake for hours after retiring to bed, pondering the events of the day which had just closed.

The sun had gone down amid clouds and shadows; but the morrow dawned brightly. The brow of Mrs. Abercrombie was undimmed as she met her family at the breakfast-table on the next morning, and every countenance reflected its cheerful light. Even Mr. Abercrombie, who had something on his conscience that troubled him, gave back his portion of the general good feeling. Lighter far was his step as he went forth and took his way to his store. His first act on his arriving there, was, to ease his conscience of the pressure thereon, by sending for Edward Wilson, and restoring him to his place under new and better auspices.

And thus the shadows passed; yet, not wholly were they expelled. The remembrance of pain abides long after the smarting wound has healed, and the heart which has once been enveloped in shadows, never loses entirely its sense of gloomy oppression. How guarded all should be lest clouds gather upon the brow, for we know not on whose hearts may fall their shadows.

GENTLE HAND.

I DID not hear the maiden's name; but in my thought I have ever since called her "Gentle Hand." What a magic lay in her touch! It was wonderful.

When and where, it matters not now to relate—but once upon a time as I was passing through a thinly peopled district of country, night came down upon me, almost unawares. Being on foot, I could not hope to gain the village toward which my steps were directed, until a late hour; and I therefore preferred seeking shelter and a night's lodging at the first humble dwelling that presented itself.

Dusky twilight was giving place to deeper shadows, when I found myself in the vicinity of a dwelling, from the small uncurtained windows of which the light shone with a pleasant promise of good cheer and comfort. The house stood within an enclosure, and a short distance from the road along which I was moving with wearied feet. Turning aside, and passing through an ill-hung gate, I approached the dwelling. Slowly the gate swung on its wooden hinges, and the rattle of its latch, in closing, did not disturb the air until I had nearly reached the little porch in front of the house, in which a slender girl, who had noticed my entrance, stood awaiting my arrival.

A deep, quick bark answered, almost like an echo, the sound of the shutting gate, and, sudden as an apparition, the form of an immense dog loomed in the doorway. I was now near enough to see the savage aspect of the animal, and the gathering motion of his body, as he prepared to bound forward upon me. His wolfish growl was really fearful. At the instant when he was about to spring, a light hand was laid upon his shaggy neck, and a low word spoken.

"Don't be afraid. He won't hurt you," said a voice, that to me sounded very sweet and musical.

I now came forward, but in some doubt as to the young girl's power over the beast, on whose rough neck her almost childish hand still lay. The dog did not seem by any means reconciled to my approach, and growled wickedly his dissatisfaction.

"Go in, Tiger," said the girl, not in a voice of authority yet in her gentle tones was the consciousness that she would be obeyed; and, as she spoke, she lightly bore upon the animal with her hand, and he turned away, and disappeared within the dwelling.

"Who's that?" A rough voice asked the question; and now a heavy-looking man took the dog's place in the door.

"Who are you? What's wanted?" There was something very harsh and forbidding in the way the man spoke. The girl now laid her hand upon his arm, and leaned, with a gentle pressure, against him.

"How far is it to G——?" I asked, not deeming it best to say, in the beginning, that I sought a resting-place for the night.

"To G——!" growled the man, but not so harshly as at first. "It's good six miles from here."

"A long distance; and I'm a stranger, and on foot," said I. "If you can make room for me until morning, I will be very thankful."

I saw the girl's hand move quickly up his arm, until it rested on his shoulder, and now she leaned to him still closer.

"Come in. We'll try what can be done for you."

There was a change in the man's voice that made me wonder.

I entered a large room, in which blazed a brisk fire. Before the fire sat two stout lads, who turned upon me their heavy eyes, with no very welcome greeting. A middle-aged woman was standing at a table, and two children were amusing themselves with a kitten on the floor.

"A stranger, mother," said the man who had given me so rude a greeting at the door; "and he wants us to let him stay all night."

The woman looked at me doubtingly for a few moments, and then replied coldly—

"We don't keep a public-house."

"I'm aware of that, ma'am," said I; "but night has overtaken me, and it's a long way yet to G——."

"Too far for a tired man to go on foot," said the master of the house, kindly, "so it's no use talking about it, mother; we must give him a bed."

So unobtrusively, that I scarcely noticed the movement, the girl had drawn to the woman's side. What she said to her, I did not hear, for the brief words were uttered in a low voice; but I noticed, as she spoke, one small, fair hand rested on the woman's hand. Was there magic in that gentle touch? The woman's repulsive aspect changed into one of kindly welcome, and she said:

"Yes, it's a long way to G——. I guess we can find a place for him. Have you had any supper?"

I answered in the negative.

The woman, without further remark, drew a pine table from the wall, placed upon it some cold meat, fresh bread and butter, and a pitcher of new milk. While these preparations were going on, I had more leisure for minute observation. There was a singular contrast between the young girl I have mentioned and the other inmates of the room; and yet, I could trace a strong likeness between the maiden and the woman, whom I supposed to be her mother—browned and hard as were the features of the latter.

Soon after I had commenced eating my supper, the two children who were playing on the floor, began quarrelling with each other.

"John! go off to bed!" said the father, in a loud, peremptory voice, speaking to one of the children.

But John, though he could not help hearing, did not choose to obey.

"Do you hear me, sir? Off with you!" repeated the angry father.

"I don't want to go," whined the child.

"Go, I tell you, this minute!"

Still, there was not the slightest movement to obey; and the little fellow looked the very image of rebellion. At this crisis in the affair, when a storm seemed inevitable, the sister, as I supposed her to be, glided across the room, and stooping down, took the child's hands in hers. Not a word was said; but the young rebel was instantly subdued. Rising, he passed out by her side, and I saw no more of him during the evening.

Soon after I had finished my supper, a neighbour came in, and it was not long before he and the man of the house were involved in a warm political discussion, in which were many more assertions than reasons. My host was not a very clear-headed man; while his antagonist was wordy and specious. The former, as might be supposed, very naturally became excited, and, now and then, indulged himself in rather strong expressions toward his neighbour, who, in turn, dealt back wordy blows that were quite as heavy as he had received, and a good deal more irritating.

And now I marked again the power of that maiden's gentle hand. I did not notice her movement to her father's side. She was there when I first observed her, with one hand laid upon his temple, and lightly smoothing the hair with a caressing motion. Gradually the high tone of then disputant subsided, and his words had in them less of personal rancour. Still, the discussion went on; and I noticed that the maiden's hand, which rested on the temple when unimpassioned words were spoken, resumed its caressing motion the instant there was the smallest perceptible tone of anger in the father's voice. It was a beautiful sight; and I could but look on and wonder at the power of that touch, so light and unobtrusive, yet possessing a spell over the hearts of all around her. As she stood there, she looked like an angel of peace, sent to still the turbulent waters of human passion. Sadly out of place, I could not but think her, amid the rough and rude; and yet, who more than they need the softening and humanizing influences of one like the Gentle Hand.

Many times more, during that evening, did I observe the magic power of her hand and voice—the one gentle yet potent as the other.

On the next morning, breakfast being over, I was preparing to take my departure, when my host informed me that if I would wait for half an hour he would give me a ride in his wagon to G——, as business required him to go there. I was very well pleased to accept of the invitation. In due time, the farmer's wagon was driven into the road before the house, and I was invited to get in. I noticed the horse as a rough-looking Canadian pony, with a certain air of stubborn endurance. As the farmer took his seat by my side, the family came to the door to see us off.

"Dick!" said the farmer, in a peremptory voice, giving the rein a quick jerk as he spoke.

But Dick moved not a step.

"Dick! you vagabond! get up." And the farmer's whip cracked sharply by the pony's ear.

It availed not, however, this second appeal. Dick stood firmly disobedient. Next the whip was brought down upon him, with an impatient hand; but the pony only reared up a little. Fast and sharp the strokes were next dealt to the number of a half-dozen. The man might as well have beaten his wagon, for all his end was gained.

A stout lad now came out into the road, and catching Dick by the bridle, jerked him forward, using, at the same time, the customary language on such occasions, but Dick met this new ally with increased stubbornness, planting his forefeet more firmly, and at a sharper angle with the ground. The impatient boy now struck the pony on the side of his head with his clenched hand, and jerked cruelly at his bridle. It availed nothing, however; Dick was not to be wrought upon by any such arguments.

"Don't do so, John!" I turned my head as the maiden's sweet voice reached my ear. She was passing through the gate into the road, and, in the next moment, had taken hold of the lad and drawn him away from the animal. No strength was exerted in this; she took hold of his arm, and he obeyed her wish as readily as if he had no thought beyond her gratification.

And now that soft hand was laid gently on the pony's neck, and a single low word spoken. How instantly were the tense muscles relaxed—how quickly the stubborn air vanished.

"Poor Dick!" said the maiden, as she stroked his neck lightly, or softly patted it with a child-like hand.

"Now, go along, you provoking fellow!" she added, in a half-chiding, yet affectionate voice, as she drew upon the bridle. The pony turned toward her, and rubbed his head against her arm for an instant or two; then, pricking up his ears, he started off at a light, cheerful trot, and went on his way as freely as if no silly crotchet had ever entered his stubborn brain.

"What a wonderful power that hand possesses!" said I, speaking to my companion, as we rode away.

He looked at me for a moment as if my remark had occasioned surprise. Then a light came into his countenance, and he said, briefly—

"She's good! Everybody and every thing loves her."

Was that, indeed, the secret of her power? Was the quality of her soul perceived in the impression of her hand, even by brute beasts! The father's explanation was, doubtless, the true one. Yet have I ever since wondered, and still do wonder, at the potency which lay in that maiden's magic touch. I have seen something of the same power, showing itself in the loving and the good, but never to the extent as instanced in her, whom, for a better name, I must still call "Gentle Hand."

A gentle touch, a soft word. Ah! how few of us, when the will is strong with its purpose, can believe in the power of agencies so apparently insignificant! And yet all great influences effect their ends silently, unobtrusively, and with a force that seems at first glance to be altogether inadequate. Is there not a lesson for us all in this?

WILL IT PAY?

"I WANT an hour of your time this morning," said Mr. Smith, as he entered the counting-room of his neighbour, Mr. Jones.

"Will it pay?" inquired Mr. Jones, smiling.

"Not much profit in money," was answered.

Mr. Jones shrugged his shoulders, and arched his eye-brows.

"Time is money," said he.

"But money isn't the all-in-all of life. There's something else in the world besides dollars."

"Oh yes; and the man that has the dollars can command as much of this 'something else' that you speak of as he pleases."

"I'm not so sure of that," replied Mr. Smith. "I can tell you something that money will not procure."

"Say on."

"A contented mind."

"I'll take that risk at a very low percentage, so far as I am concerned," answered Mr. Jones.

"But, as to this hour of my time that you ask? What is the object?"

"You remember Lloyd who used to do business on the wharf?"

"Yes; what of him? I thought he died in New Orleans a year ago."

"So he did."

"Not worth a dollar!"

"Not worth many dollars, I believe. He was never a very shrewd man, so far as business was concerned, though honourable and kind-hearted. He did not prosper after leaving our city."

"Honourable and kind-hearted!" returned Mr. Jones, with a slight air of contempt. "Such men are as plenty as blackberries. I can point them out to you by the dozen in every square; but it does not pay to be on too intimate terms with them."

"Why?"

"You are very apt to suffer through their amiable weaknesses."

"Is this your experience?" inquired Mr. Smith.

"My experience is not very extensive in that line, I flatter myself," said Mr. Jones; "but I know of some who have suffered."

"I was speaking of Mr. Lloyd."

"Yes—what of him?"

"I learned this morning that his widow arrived in our city yesterday, and that she needs friendly aid and counsel. It seems to me that those who knew and esteemed her husband ought not to regard her with indifference. I propose to call upon her and inquire as to her needs and purposes, and I want you to accompany me."

"Can't do it," answered Mr. Jones, very promptly.

"Why not?"

"It won't pay," returned Mr. Jones.

"I don't expect it to pay in a business sense," said Mr. Smith; "but, surely, humanity has some claim to consideration."

"Humanity! humph. Humanity don't pay, Mr. Smith; that's my experience. I've helped two or three in my time, and what return do you suppose I received?"

"The pleasing consciousness of having done good to your neighbour."

"Not a bit of it. I lost my money for my pains, and made enemies into the bargain. When I demanded my own, I received only insult—that's my experience, Mr. Smith, and the experience of ninety-nine in a hundred who listen to the so-called claims of humanity. As I said before—it doesn't pay."

"Then you will not go with me to see Mrs. Lloyd?"

"No, sir. You don't catch me hunting up the widows of broken merchants. Let them go to their own friends. I'd soon have plenty of rather unprofitable business on my hands, if I were to engage in affairs of this kind."

"I hardly think it will pay to talk with you on this subject any longer," said Mr. Smith.

"I'm just of your opinion," was the laughing answer, "unless I can induce you to let Mrs. Lloyd remain in ignorance of your benevolent intentions, and mind your own concerns, like a sensible man."

"Good morning," said Mr. Smith.

"Good morning," replied Jones; "in a week or two I shall expect to hear your report on this widow-hunting expedition."

"It will pay, I reckon," said Mr. Smith, as he passed from the store.

"Pay," muttered Jones, a sneer now curling his lip, "he'll have to pay, and roundly, too, unless more fortunate than he deserves to be."

A little while after the departure of Mr. Smith, a sallow, sharp-featured man, with a restless eye, entered the store of Mr. Jones.

"Ah, Perkins!" said the latter, familiarly, "any thing afloat to-day?"

"Well, yes, there is; I know of one operation that is worth looking at."

"Will it pay, friend Perkins? That's the touchstone with me. Show me any thing that will pay, and I'm your man for a trade."

"I can get you fifty shares of Riverland Railroad stock, at eighty-two!"

"Can you?" The face of Jones brightened.

"I can."

"All right. I'll take it."

"Give me your note at sixty days, and I'll have the shares transferred at once."

In five minutes from the time Perkins entered the store of Mr. Jones, he left with the merchant's note for over four thousand dollars in his hand. The shares in the Riverland Railroad had been steadily advancing for some months, and Mr. Jones entertained not the shadow of a doubt that in a very short period they would be up to par. He had already purchased freely, and at prices beyond eighty-two dollars. The speculation he regarded as entirely safe, and one that would "pay" handsomely.

"I think that will pay a good deal better than hunting up the poor widows of insolvent merchants," said Mr. Jones to himself, as he walked the length of his store once or twice, rubbing his hands every now and then with irrepressible glee. "If I'd been led off by Smith on that fool's errand, just see what I would have lost. Operations like that don't go a begging long. But this gentleman knows in what quarter his interest lies."

Not long after the departure of Perkins, a small wholesale dealer, named Armor, came into the store of Mr. Jones.

"I have several lots that I am anxious to close out this morning," said he. "Can I do any thing here?"

"What have you?" asked Mr. Jones.

"Ten boxes of tobacco, fifty prime hams, ten boxes Havana cigars, some rice, &c."

Now, these were the very articles Mr. Jones wanted, and which he would have to purchase in a day or two. But he affected indifference as he inquired the price. The current market rates were mentioned.

"No temptation," said Mr. Jones, coldly.

"They are prime articles, all; none better to be had," said the dealer.

"If I was in immediate want of them, I could give you an order; but"——

"Will you make me an offer?" inquired Armor, somewhat earnestly. "I have a good deal of money to raise to-day, and for cash will sell at a bargain."

Mr. Jones mused for some time. He was not certain whether, in making or requiring an offer, he would get the best bargain out of his needy customer. At last he said—

"Put down your prices to the very lowest figure, and I can tell you at a word whether I will close out these lots for you. As I said before, I have a good stock of each on hand."

For what a small gain will some men sacrifice truth and honour!

The dealer had notes in bank that must be lifted, and he saw no way of obtaining all the funds he needed, except through forced sales, at a depression on the market prices. So, to make certain of an operation, he named, accordingly, low rates—considerably below cost.

Mr. Jones, who was very cunning, and very shrewd, accepted the prices on two or three articles, but demurred to the rest, and these the most important of the whole. Finally, an operation was made, in which he was a gainer, in the purchase of goods for which he had almost immediate sale, of over two hundred dollars, while the needy merchant was a loser by just that sum.

"That paid!" was the self-congratulatory ejaculation of Mr. Jones, "and handsomely, too. I should like to do it over again, about a dozen times before night. Rather better than widow speculations—ha! ha!"

We shall see. On leaving the store of his neighbour, Mr. Smith went to the hotel at which he understood Mrs. Lloyd had taken lodgings, and made inquiry for her. A lady in deep mourning, accompanied by two daughters, one a lovely girl, not over twenty years of age, and the other about twelve, soon entered the parlour.

"Mrs. Lloyd, I believe," said Mr. Smith.

The lady bowed. As soon as all parties were seated, the gentleman said—

"My name is Smith. During your former residence in this city, I was well acquainted with your husband. Permit me to offer my heartfelt sympathy in the painful bereavement you have suffered."

There was a slight pause, and then Mr. Smith resumed—

"Hearing of your return to this city, I have called to ask if there are any good offices that I can render you. If you have any plans for the future—if you want advice—if a friend in need will be of service—do not hesitate to speak freely, My high regard for your husband's memory will not suffer me to be indifferent to the welfare of his widow and children."

Mr. Smith had not purposed making, when he called, so general a tender of service. But there was something in the lady's fine countenance which told him that she had both independence and decision of character, and that he need not fear an abuse of his generous kindness.

Touched by such an unexpected declaration, it was some moments before she could reply. She then said—

"I thank you, in the name of my departed husband, for this unlooked-for and generous offer. Though back in the city, which was formerly my home, I find myself comparatively a stranger. Yesterday I made inquiry for Mr. Edward Hunter, an old and fast friend of Mr. Lloyd's, and to my pain and regret learned that he was deceased."

"Yes, madam; he died about two months ago."

"With him I purposed consulting as to my future course of action; but his death has left me without a single friend in the city to whose judgment I can confide my plans and purposes."

"Mr. Hunter was one of nature's noblemen," said Mr. Smith, warmly; "and you are not the only one who has cause to mourn his loss. But there are others in our city who are not insensible to the claims of humanity—others who, like him, sometimes let their thoughts range beyond the narrow sphere of self."

"My object in returning to this place," resumed Mrs. Lloyd, "was to get started in some safe and moderately profitable business. A short time before my husband's removal, by the death of a distant relative I fell heir to a small piece of landed property, which I recently sold in New Orleans. By the advice of my agent there, I have invested the money in fifty shares of Riverland Railroad stock, which he said I could sell here at a good advance. These shares are now in the hands of a broker, named Perkins, who is authorized to sell them at eighty-two dollars a share."

"He'll find no difficulty in doing that, ma'am. I would have taken them at eighty-three."

At this stage of the conversation, Perkins himself entered the parlour.

"Ah, Mr. Smith!" said he, "I called at your place of business this morning, but was not so fortunate as to find you in. I had fifty shares of Riverland stock, the property of Mrs. Lloyd here, which I presumed you would like to buy."

"You were not out of the way in your presumption. Have you made the sale?"

"Oh yes. Not finding you in, I saw Mr. Jones, who took the shares at a word."

"At what price?"

"Eighty-two. I have his note at sixty days for the amount, which you know is perfectly good."

"Mrs. Lloyd need not have the slightest hesitation in accepting it; and if she wishes the money, I can get it cashed for her." Then rising, he added, "I will leave you now, Mrs. Lloyd, as business requires both your attention and mine. To-morrow I will do myself the pleasure to call on you again."

As Mr. Smith bowed himself out, he noticed, more particularly, the beautiful smile of the elder daughter, whose eyes, humid from grateful emotion, were fixed on his countenance with an expression that haunted him for hours afterward.

"I hardly think that paid," was the remark of Mr. Jones, on meeting Mr. Smith some hours afterward.

"What?" asked the latter.

"Your visit to Lloyd's widow."

"Why do you say so?"

"You lost a bargain which came into my hands, and on which I could get an advance of a hundred dollars to-morrow."

"Ah, what was it?"

"Perkins had fifty shares of Riverland stock, which he was authorized to sell at eighty-two. He called on you first; but instead of being on hand, in business hours, you were off on a charity expedition. So the ripe cherry dropped into my open mouth. I told you it wouldn't pay, neighbour Smith."

"And yet it has paid, notwithstanding your prophecy," said Smith.

"It has!"

"Yes."

"In what way?"

But Mr. Smith was not disposed to cast his pearls before swine, and so evaded the direct question. He knew that his mercenary neighbour would trample under foot, with sneering contempt, any expression of the pure satisfaction he derived from what he had done—would breathe upon and obscure the picture of a grateful mother and her daughter, if he attempted to elevate it before his eyes. It had paid, but beyond this he did not seek to enlighten his fellow-merchant.

Three days later, Mr. Jones is at his desk, buried in calculations of profit and loss, and so much absorbed is he, that he has not noticed the entrance of Perkins the broker, through whom he obtained the stock from Mrs. Lloyd.

"How much of the Riverland Railroad stock have you?" inquired the broker, and in a voice that sent a sudden fear to the heart of the merchant.

"A hundred shares. Why do you ask?" was the quick response.

"I'm sorry for you, then. The interest due this day is not forthcoming."

"What!" Mr. Jones starts from his desk, his lips pale and quivering.

"There's something wrong in the affairs of the company, it is whispered. At any rate, the interest won't be paid, and the stock has tumbled down to thirty-five dollars. If you'll take my advice you'll sell. The first loss is usually the best in these cases—that is my experience."

It is very plain that one operation hasn't paid, for all its golden promise—an operation that would hardly have been effected by Mr. Jones, had he accompanied Mr. Smith on the proposed visit to Mrs. Lloyd. The fifty shares of stock, which came, as he thought, so luckily into his hand, would, in all probability, have become the property of another.

And not a week glided by ere Mr. Jones became aware of the fact that another operation had failed to pay. A cargo of coffee and sugar arrived one morning; the vessel containing it had been looked for daily, and Mr. Jones fully expected to receive the consignment; he was not aware of the arrival until he met the captain in the street.

"Captain Jackson! How are you? This is really an unexpected pleasure!" exclaimed the merchant, as he grasped the hand of the individual he addressed, and shook it warmly.

Captain Jackson did not seem equally gratified at meeting the merchant. He took his hand coldly, and scarcely smiled in return.

"When did you arrive?" asked Mr. Jones.

"This morning."

"Indeed! I was not aware of it. For over a week I have been expecting you."

The captain merely bowed.

"Will you be around to my store this afternoon?" asked Mr. Jones.

"I presume not."

There was now, on the part of Mr. Jones, an embarrassed pause. Then he said —

"Shall I have the sale of your cargo?"

"No, sir," was promptly and firmly answered.

"I have made the consignment to Armor."

"To Armor!" exclaimed Mr. Jones, in ill-concealed surprise.

"He's a perfectly fair man, is he not?" said the captain.

"Oh yes. Perfectly fair. He'll do you justice, without doubt. Still I must own to being a little disappointed, you were satisfied with the way your business was done last time."

"Not altogether, Mr. Jones," said Captain Jackson. "You were a little too sharp for, me—rather too eager, in securing your own advantage, to look narrowly enough to mine. Such was my impression, and it has, been confirmed since my arrival this morning."

"That's a grave charge, Captain Jackson," said Mr. Jones; "You must explain yourself."

"I'm a plain spoken, and a straightforward sort of a man, sir." The captain drew himself up, and looked particularly dignified. "The truth is, as I have said, I thought you were rather too sharp for me the last time. But I determined to try you once more, and to watch you as closely as a cat watches a mouse. I was on my way to your store, when I met an old friend, in business here, and, put to him the direct question as to what he thought of your fairness in trade. 'He's sharp,' was the answer. 'He will not take an undue advantage?' said I. 'Your idea as to what constitutes an undue advantage would hardly agree with that of Mr. Jones,' replied my friend. And then he related the circumstance of your finding Armor in a tight place last week, and getting from him a lot of goods for two hundred dollars less than they were worth. I went to Armor, and, on his confirming the statement, at once placed my cargo in his hands. The commissions will repair his loss, and give him a few hundred dollars over. I'm afraid of men who are too sharp in dealing. Are you satisfied with my explanation?"

"Good morning, sir," said Mr. Jones.

"Good morning," returned, Captain Jackson. And bowing formally, the two men separated.

"That didn't pay," muttered Jones between his teeth, as he moved on with his eyes cast to the ground, even in his chagrin and mortification using his favourite word—

"No, it, didn't pay," And, in truth, no operations of this kind do really pay. They may seem to secure advantage, but always result in loss—if not in lose of money, in loss of that which should be dearer to a man than all the wealth of the Indies—his self-respect and virtuous integrity of character.

On the evening of that day, a pleasant little company was assembled at the house of Mr. Smith, made up of the merchant's own family and three guests—Mrs. Lloyd and her daughters. Through the advice of Mr. Smith, and by timely action on his part, a house of moderate capacity had been secured, at a great bargain, for the sum of three thousand dollars, to which it was proposed to remove, as soon as furniture, on the way from New Orleans, should arrive. The first story of this house was already fitted up as a store; and, as the object of Mrs. Lloyd was to get into business in a small way, the purchase of the property was made, in order as well to obtain a good location as to make a safe investment. With the thousand dollars that remained, it was proposed to lay in a small stock of fancy dry-goods.

In the few interviews held with Mrs. Lloyd by the merchant, he was struck with the beautiful harmony of her character, and especially with her womanly dignity. As for the eldest daughter, something about her had charmed him from the very beginning. And now when, for the first time, this interesting family were his guests for a social evening—when he saw their characters in a new aspect—and when he felt, through the quick sympathy of a generous nature, how grateful and happy they were—he experienced a degree of satisfaction such as never pervaded the breast of any man whose love of mere gain was the measure of his good-will toward others.

How different was the social sphere in the house of Mr. Jones on that evening! The brow of the husband and father was clouded, and his lips sealed in silence; or if words were spoken, they were in moody tones, or uttered in fretfulness and ill-nature. The wife and children caught from him the same repulsive spirit, and, in their intercourse one with the other, found little sympathy or affection. There was a chilling shadow on the household of the merchant; it fell from the monster form of his expanding selfishness, that was uplifted between the sunlight of genuine humanity and the neighbour he would not regard. Alas! on how many thousands and thousands of households in our own land rests the gigantic shadow of this monster!

"Will it pay?" is the eager question we hear on all sides, as we mingle in the business world.

"Has it paid?" Ah, that is the after-question! Reader, is the monster's shadow in your household? If so, it has not paid.

THE LAY PREACHER.

WHETHER the Rev. Andrew Adkin had or had not a call to preach, is more than we can say. Enough, that he considered it his duty to "hold forth" occasionally on the Sabbath; and when "Brother Adkin" saw, in any possible line of action, his duty, he never took counsel of Jonah.

Brother Adkin kept a store in the town of Mayberry, and being a man of some force of character, and not, by any means, indifferent to this world's goods, devoted himself to business during the six days of the week with commendable assiduity. It is not the easiest thing in the world to banish, on the Sabbath, all concern in regard to business. Most persons engaged in trade, no matter how religiously inclined, have experienced this difficulty. Brother Adkin's case did, not prove an exception; and so intrusive, often, were these worldly thoughts and cares, that they desecrated, at times, the pulpit, making the good man's voice falter and his hands tremble, as he endeavoured, "in his feeble way," to break the bread of life.

He had his own trials and temptations—his own stern "exercises of mind," going to the extent, not unfrequently, of startling doubts as to the reality of his call to preach.

"I don't see much fruit of my labour," he would sometimes say to himself, "and I often think I do more harm than good."

Such thoughts, however, were usually disposed of, as suggestions of the "adversary."

A week in the life of Brother Adkin will show the peculiar influences that acted upon him, and how far his secular pursuits interfered with and marred his usefulness as a preacher.

Monday morning had come round again. He had preached twice on the Sabbath—once to a strange congregation, and with apparent good effect, and once to a congregation in Mayberry. In the latter case, he was favoured with little freedom of utterance. The beginning of the secular week brought back to the mind of Mr. Adkin the old current of thought, and the old earnest desire to get gain in business. On the Sabbath he had taught the people that love was the fulfilment of the law,—now, he had regard only to his own interests; and, although he did not adopt the broad, unscrupulous maxim, that all is fair in trade, yet, in every act of buying and selling, the thought uppermost in his mind was, the amount of gain to be received in the transaction.

"What are you paying for corn to-day?" asked a man, a stranger to Mr. Adkin.

"Forty-eight cents," was answered.

"Is this the highest market rate?" said the man.

"I bought fifty bushels at that price on Saturday," replied Mr. Adkin.

Now, since Saturday, the price of corn had advanced four cents, and Mr. Adkin knew it. But he thought he would just try his new customer with the old price, and if he chose to sell at that, why there would be so much gained.

"I have forty bushels," said the man.

"Very well, I'll take it at forty-eight cents. Where is it?"

"My wagon is at the tavern."

"You may bring it over at once. My man is now at leisure to attend to the delivery."

The corn was delivered and paid for, and both parties, for the time being, were well satisfied with the transaction.

The day had nearly run to a close, and Mr. Adkin was in the act of estimating his gains, when the man from whom he had purchased the corn entered his store.

"Look here, my friend," said the latter speaking rather sharply, "you paid me too little for that corn."

"How so?" returned Mr. Adkin, in well-affected surprise.

"You was to pay the highest market price," said the man.

"I offered you forty-eight cents."

"And I asked you if that was the highest rate, didn't I?"

"I told you that I had bought fifty bushels at that price on Saturday."

"Oh, ho! Now I comprehend you," said the man, with a sarcastic curl of his lip. "I was recommended to you as a preacher, and one who would deal fairly with me. I asked you a plain question, and you purposely misled me in your answer, to the end that you might get my corn at less than the market value. You have cheated me out of nearly two dollars. Much good may it do you!"

And saying this, he turned on his heel and left the store. Mr. Adkin was, of course, no little disturbed. The charge of dishonesty in dealing at first aroused his indignation; but as he grew calmer and thought over the affair, his conscience troubled him. As a Christian man, and especially as a Christian minister, he could not reconcile his dealing with strict gospel requirements.

The more he reflected, the more closely he brought his conduct to the standard of Christian principles, the less was he satisfied with himself. The final result was, a determination to go to the man on the next morning, and pay him the balance due him on the market price of his corn. But, when he sought for him, he was not to be found, having gone back to his home, a few miles from the village.

On the next day he sent for a bill, which had been standing a good while. His clerk brought back some impertinent and altogether unsatisfactory answer.

"Did Mr. Giles say that?" he asked, his eyes flashing indignantly.

"His exact words," replied the clerk.

"Very well. I'll not send to him again," said Mr. Adkin. "He thinks, because I am a preacher, that he can treat me as he pleases, but I'll let him know that being a preacher doesn't make me any the less a man, nor any the less inclined to protect myself."

So Mr. Giles was served with a summons, to answer for debt, before the week was out.

On the day following, a certain lady, a member of the congregation in Mayberry to which he preached, whenever, from sickness or other causes, the regular minister was absent, came into Mr. Adkin's store. Her manner was considerably excited.

"There's a mistake in your bill, Mr. Adkin," said she, in rather a sharp tone of voice.

"If so, Mrs. Smith, the remedy is a very simple one," replied Mr. Adkin. Her manner had disturbed him, yet he concealed the disturbance under a forced suavity of manner. "Where does the mistake lie?"

"Why, see here. You've got me charged with six yards of muslin and five pounds of butter that I never got!"

"Are you certain of this, Mrs. Smith?"

"Certain! Be sure I'm certain! D'ye think I'd say I hadn't the things, if I had them? I'm not quite so bad as that, Mr. Adkin!"

"Don't get excited about the matter, Mrs. Smith. We are all liable to mistakes. There's an error here, either on your side or mine, if it is my error, I will promptly correct it."

"Of course it's your error. I never had either the muslin or the butter," said Mrs. Smith, positively.

Mr. Adkin turned to his ledger, where Mrs. Smith's account was posted.

"The muslin is charged on the 10th of June."

Mrs. Smith looked at the bill and answered affirmatively.

"You bought a pound of yarn and a straw hat on the same day."

"Yes; I remember them. But I didn't get the muslin."

"Think again, Mrs. Smith. Don't you remember the beautiful piece of Merrimac that I showed you, and how cheap you thought it?"

"I never had six yards of muslin, Mr. Adkin."

"But, Mrs. Smith, I have distinct recollection of measuring it off, and the charge is here in my own handwriting."

"I never had it, Mr. Adkin!" said the lady much excited.

"You certainly had, Mrs. Smith."

"I'll never pay for it!"

"Don't say that, Mrs. Smith. You certainly wouldn't want my goods without paying for them!"

"I never had the muslin, I tell you!"

Argument in the case Mr. Adkin found to be useless. The sale of the five pounds of butter was as distinctly remembered by him; and as he was not the man to yield a right when he had no doubt as to its existence, he would not erase the articles from Mrs Smith bill, which was paid under protest.

"It's the last cent you'll ever get of my money!" said Mrs. Smith, as she handed over, the amount of the bill. "I never had those articles; and I shall always say that I was wronged out of so much money."

"I'm sure, madam, I don't want your custom, if I'm expected to let you have my goods for nothing," retorted Mr. Adkin, the natural man in him growing strong under an allegation that implied dishonesty.

So the two parted, neither feeling good-will toward the other, and neither being in a very composed state of mind.

Each day in that week brought something to disturb the mind of Mr. Adkin; and each day brought him into unpleasant business contact with someone in the town of Mayberry. To avoid, these things was almost impossible, particularly for a man of Mr. Adkin's temperament.

Saturday night came, always a busy night for the storekeeper. It was ten o'clock, and customers were still coming in, when a lad handed Mr. Adkin a note, it was from the regularly stationed minister of the church in Mayberry to which Mr. Adkin belonged. The note stated, briefly, that the writer was so much indisposed, that he would not be able to preach on the next day, and conveyed the request that "Brother Adkin" would "fill the pulpit for him in the morning."

Brother Adkin almost groaned in spirit at this unwelcome and not-to-be-denied invitation to perform ministerial duties on the Sabbath. Of theological subjects, scarcely a thought had entered his mind since Monday morning; and, certainly, the states through which he had passed were little calculated to elevate his affections, or make clear his spiritual intuitions.

It was twelve o'clock before Mr. Adkin was able to retire on that night. As he rested his weary and now aching head on his pillow, he endeavoured to turn his mind from worldly things, and fix it upon things heavenly and eternal. But, the current of thought and affection had too long been flowing in another channel. The very effort to check its onward course, caused disturbance and obscurity. There was a brief but fruitless struggle, when overtaxed nature vindicated her claims, and as the lay preacher found relief from perplexing thoughts and a troubled conscience, in refreshing slumber.

In the half-dreaming, half-waking state that comes with the dawning of day, Mr. Adkin's thoughts flowed on again in the old channel, and when full consciousness came, he found himself busy with questions of profit and loss. Self-accusation and humiliation followed. He "wrote bitter things against himself," for this involuntary desecration of the Sabbath.

Rising early, he took his Bible, and after turning over book after book and scanning chapter after chapter, finally chose a verse as the text from which he would preach. Hurriedly and imperfectly our lay preacher conned his subject. Clearness of discrimination, grasp of thought, orderly arrangement, were out of the question. That would have been too much for a master mind, under similar circumstances.

Eleven o'clock came around quickly, and painfully conscious of an obscure and confused state of mind, Mr. Adkin entered the house of God and ascended the pulpit. A little while he sat, endeavouring to collect his thoughts; then he arose and commenced giving out a hymn. Lifting his eyes from the book, as he finished reading the first verse, he saw, directly in front of him, the man from whom he had purchased the forty bushels of corn. He was looking at him fixedly, and there was on his countenance an expression of surprise and contempt, that, bringing back, as the man's presence did, a vivid recollection of the events of Monday, almost deprived Mr. Adkin, for a moment or two, of utterance. He faltered, caught his breath, and went on again with the reading. On raising his eyes at the conclusion of the second verse, Mr. Adkin saw his corn customer slowly moving down the aisle toward the door of entrance. How keenly he felt the rebuke! How sadly conscious was he of being out of place in the pulpit!

After the singing of the hymn, the preacher made a prayer; but it was cold and disjointed. He had no freedom of utterance. A chapter was read, an anthem sung, and then Mr. Adkin arose in the pulpit, took his text, and, ere giving utterance to the first words of his discourse, let his eyes wander over the congregation. A little to the right sat Mr. Giles, wearing a very sober aspect of countenance, and looking at him with knit brows and compressed lips. The sight caused the words "brother going to law with brother" to pass almost electrically through his mind. As his glance rebounded from Mr. Giles quickly, it next rested upon Mrs. Smith, who, with perked head and a most malicious curling of the lip, said, as plain as manner could say it—"You're a nice man for a preacher, a'n't you?"

How Mr. Adkin beat about the bushes and wrought in obscurity, darkening counsel by words without knowledge, during the half hour that followed the enunciation of his text, need not here be told. None was more fully conscious than himself of his utter failure to give spiritual instruction to the waiting congregation. The climax, so far as he was concerned, was yet to come. As he descended the pulpit stairs, at the close of the service, some one slipped a piece of paper into his hand. Glancing at the pencilled writing thereon, he read the rebuking words:

"The hungry sheep look up, and are not fed."

How could he feed them? Are holy and divine things of such easy comprehension, that a man may devote the whole energies of his mind to worldly business during six days, and then become a lucid expounder of heavenly, mysteries on the Sabbath? The influx of intelligence into the mind of a speaker, is in exact ratio with the knowledge he has acquired. He may have, without this previous preparation, "free utterance," as it is called; but this utterance brings no rational convictions; it sways only by the power of contagious enthusiasm. Moreover, as in the case of Mr. Adkin, every lay preacher takes with him into the pulpit a taint from worldly and business contact, and his presence there must turn the thoughts of many hearers from his clerical to his personal character—from the truth he enunciates, to his practical observance thereof in daily life. He may be judged falsely; but the fact of his blending the two separate characters of clergyman and layman, forms an occasion for false judgment, and detracts from the usefulness of the sacred office.

Whether Mr. Adkin "held forth" again, we cannot apprize the reader. New light, and new perceptions of duty certainly came into his mind; and we may hope that, as he was a well-meaning and conscientious man, he was led to act wisely in the future.

Having given a true picture of a week in the life of the lay preacher, our business with him is done. It is for those whom it may concern to study the sketch, and see if it does not contain some points worthy their especial consideration.

HOW TO DESTROY A GOOD BUSINESS.
CHAPTER I.

"WELL, Mr. Tompkins, what do you think about it? I wish you would speak. I've been talking at you for full ten blessed minutes, and you haven't as much as opened your lips in reply."

"About what?" asked Mr. Tompkins, looking up with an air of surprise.

"About what, indeed!" rejoined the lady, in no very melodious tone. "Why, about that house in Franklin Street, to be sure. What else did you suppose it was?"

"Oh! ah! yes."

"Mr. Tompkins, why don't you answer me like a man? Oh! ah! yes! I hate that."

"Humph!"

"Yes, and I hate that just as bad. But you needn't think to put me off with a 'humph!' Have you made up your mind about buying that house—say?"

"I've got to make up my mind about something else first."

"Indeed! And what is that, pray?"

"About where the money is to come from."

"Mr. Tompkins, I am out of all patience with you! Its precious little that I ask for, dear knows! But even that little is never granted."

"If you'll get me the money, Ellen, I'll buy the house with pleasure," returned Mr. Tompkins, in a quiet voice.

"Me! I wonder where I'd get the money? It's an insult for you to talk to me in this way, when you keep me as poor as a church mouse all the time. Every dollar I get from you is like pulling a tooth."

"And causes me as much pain, sometimes."

"I won't put up with such treatment from you, Mr. Tompkins," said the good lady, passionately, and walked from the room with a stately step and an effort at dignity. The husband retreated precipitately, and sought his place of business. He sighed as he took his seat upon a counting-house stool at the desk, and commenced turning over the pages of various large account-books. While thus engaged, a person entered his store, and was shown back to that portion of it where he had retired. Mr. Tompkins looked up on hearing his name pronounced, and met the steady eye of one whose presence was not very agreeable to him just at that time.

"Ah, Mr. Wolford! How are you to-day? I am glad to see you," he said, with an effort to seem pleased and indifferent.

"Very well. How are you?" was the blunt response.

"Take a chair, Mr. Wolford."

The visitor sat down, with considerable emphasis in his manner, threw one leg over the other, and leaned back in his chair. Tompkins was nervous. His effort to seem at ease led him into overaction.

He smiled, or rather smirked—for a smile is always natural, never forced—and introduced various topics of conversation, one after the other, with the manner of a man whose thoughts were far away from his words, and who yet wished to be very agreeable to a personage from whom he wished a favour.

"What do you think of the news from Washington to-day, Mr. Wolford? Strange doings there!"

"Rather."

"Our party were completely outgeneralled in that measure."

"Yes."

"Bad news from London."

"Yes, bad enough."

"It has played the mischief with stocks."

"Thank fortune, I don't deal in stocks."

And thus Tompkins run on, and Wolford replied cold and sententiously for some ten minutes. Then there came a pause, and the two men looked into each other's faces for a short time, without either of them speaking.

"The year for which I loaned you ten thousand dollars expires next week," said Wolford, in a quiet tone, breaking the silence.

"Does it?" returned Tompkins, affecting surprise. "I had no idea the time was so near being up. Are you sure?"

"I never make mistakes in such matters, Mr. Tompkins, and can't understand how other people can."

"Creditors are said to have better memories than debtors," replied Tompkins, attempting something like pleasantry.

"Yes—I know. You will, of course, be prepared to take up the mortgage upon your property?"

"I am afraid not, Mr. Wolford. Money is exceedingly tight. But as your security is perfectly good, and you do not want the money, you will let the matter remain as it is for a little while longer?"

"I loaned you the money for a year, did I not?"

"Yes."

"Very well. The year will be up in a week."

"I would like to borrow the same amount for another year."

"I have no objection to your doing so, if you can find any one who will lend it."

"Will you not do so?"

"No. I have other use for my money."

"I will increase the interest, if that will be any inducement. Money in a good business like mine can bear a heavy interest."

"I am not satisfied with the security. Property is falling in value."

"Not satisfied!'" exclaimed Tompkins, in unfeigned surprise. "The property is worth double the sum you have advanced for my use."

"I differ with you—and I am not alone in differing."

"Very well, Mr. Wolford," said Tompkins, in a changed tone, that evinced roused and half-indignant feeling, "you shall be paid. I can easily transfer the security to some other person, if I find it necessary to do so, and raise the amount due you."

Wolford, phlegmatic as he was, seemed slightly moved by this unexpected change in the manner and position of Tompkins. He narrowly observed the expression of his face, but did not reply. He was afraid to trust himself to speak, lest he should betray his real thoughts.

"You will be prepared to pay me next week, then," he at length said, rising.

"Yes, sir. You shall have the money," replied Tompkins.

"Good day." And Wolford retired; not altogether satisfied that he had gained all he had hoped to gain by the visit.

"Ah me!" sighed Tompkins, turning to his desk as soon as this man had departed. "Here comes more trouble. That miserly wretch has no more use for his money than the man in the moon. It seems to give him delight to make every one feel his power. It is for no other reason than this, that I am now to be harassed half out of my life in order to raise ten thousand dollars in a week, besides meeting my other payments. I must try and get some one to take the mortgage he is about releasing."

While thus musing, the individual who had just left him was walking slowly down Market Street, with his eyes upon the pavement, in deep thought. He was a short, stoutly built old man, dressed in a well-worn suit of brown broadcloth. His hat was white, large in the brim, low in the crown, and pulled down so heavily on the high collar of his coat, that it turned up behind in a very decided way, indicating the save-all propensities of its owner. His face was as hard as iron: it was deeply seamed by years or the indulgence of the baser cupidities of a perverted nature. His lower lip projected slightly beyond the upper that was pressed closely upon it. His small gray eyes were deeply sunk beneath a wrinkled forehead, and twinkled like stars when any thing excited him; usually they were as calm and passionless as any part of his face.

This man had never engaged, during his whole life, in any useful branch of business. Money was the god he worshipped, and to gain this, he was ready to make almost any sacrifice. He started in life with five thousand dollars—a legacy from a distant relative. To risk this sum, or any portion of it, in trade, would have been, in his view, the most egregious folly. His first investment was in six per cent. ground-rents, from which he received three hundred dollars per annum. It cost him two hundred to live; he had, therefore, at the end of the year, a surplus of one hundred dollars. He was casting about in his mind what he should do with this in, order to make it profitable, when a hard-pressed tradesman asked him for the loan of a hundred dollars for a short time. The idea of loaning his money, when first presented, almost made his hair stand on end. He shook his head, and uttered a decided "No." It so happened that the man was so much in need of money, that he became importunate.

"I know you have it, if you would only lend it, Wolford," said he. "Let me have a hundred dollars for a month, and I will give you a good interest for it, and security besides."

"What kind of security?" eagerly asked the miser, his face brightening. The idea had struck him, as being a good one. The man was a tailor.

"I will let you hold Mr. S—— P——'s note, at six months, for one hundred and fifty dollars, as security."

Wolford shook his head.

"He might die or break, and then where would be my hundred dollars?"

"I would pay it to you."

Wolford continued to shake his head.

"How would a piece of broadcloth answer your purpose?"

"What is it worth?"

"I have a piece of twenty yards, worth eight dollars a yard. It would bring six and a half under the hammer. You can hold that, if you please."

"How much interest will you pay?"

"I will give you two dollars for the use of one hundred for thirty days."

"If you will say three, you may have it."

"Three per cent. a month!—thirty-six per cent. a year! Oh no! That would ruin any man."

"I don't think the operation worth making for less than three dollars."

"It is too much, Wolford. But I'll tell you what I'll do. Let it be for sixty days, and make the interest five dollars."

"I to hold the cloth as security until it is paid?"

"Certainly."

"Very well. You shall have the money."

A note for one hundred and five dollars, at sixty days, was drawn and handed to the young shaver, who paid down one hundred dollars, and went off with his collateral under his arm.

This transaction opened a new world to Wolford's imagination. Two and a half per cent. a month, and six per cent. per annum, could hardly be compared together. He sat down and began to figure up the result of the one operation in comparison with the other, and found that while his investment in ground-rents yielded only three hundred dollars a year, five thousand dollars, at two and a half per cent. a month, the rate at which he had made the operation just referred to, would yield fifteen hundred dollars per annum!

From that moment he became dissatisfied with ground-rents as an investment. As quickly as it could be done, he sold, for one thousand dollars, a piece of real estate, and, depositing the money in bank, looked around him for good paper to shave. He did not have to look very long. Borrowers quickly presented themselves, but no one got money except on the most tangible kind of security, and at a ruinous interest. Careful as he tried to be, Wolford was not always successful in his operations. One or two failures on the part of his borrowers, made him acquainted at a magistrate's office, where he acquired another new idea upon which he improved.

"If you wish to invest money safely and profitably, I will put you in the way of doing it," said a petty dispenser of justice to poor debtors, rogues and vagabonds, aside to the miser one day, after he had given judgment against a delinquent borrower.

"How?" eagerly asked Wolford.

"A great many cases of debt are decided by me every week, on amounts varying from one to fifty dollars," replied the magistrate. "As soon as a judgment is given, the debtor has to pay the money, find security, or go to jail, In most cases, the matter is settled by security for six months, when the debt, with costs and interest, has to be paid."

"Legal interest?" asked Wolford.

"Certainly," replied the magistrate, with a smile. "It is a legal matter, and only legal interest can be charged."

"Oh, of course! I didn't think of that."

"Very well: after a judgment is obtained, in five cases out of six the prosecutor is sick, of the business, and perfectly willing to sell out the judgment and have no more to do with it. The best business in the world is to buy these judgments. You can make at least forty per cent. per annum."

"What!"

"Forty per cent."

"Forty per cent!" and Wolford's eyes sparkled. "Are you sure?"

"Oh, yes. If I were allowed to buy them, as I am not, I would wish no better business."

"You think it safe?"

"Nothing can be safer. If the judgment is not paid at the end of six months, you can go to work immediately, with an execution, on the property of the original debtor, or his security, as you may think best, and at once obtain your money."

"Suppose neither of them have any property?"

"I take very good care not to accept bad security. Besides, you will find but few persons out of whom fifty dollars, or less, may not be obtained, under the pressure of an execution."

"I like the idea amazingly," said Wolford, thoughtfully. "Forty per cent. per annum! Capital! I will buy judgments."

"I have two hundred dollars' worth in my desk now, which I have directions to sell. Do you want them? They have six months to run. Twenty per cent. off will be just forty dollars—here they are."

Wolford carefully examined the documents which the magistrate placed in his hands, and, after considering the subject for some time, said that he would buy them. His check for one hundred and sixty dollars was received by the magistrate, and the judgments became his property.

"It's even better than forty per cent. per annum," remarked the magistrate, as he folded up the check he had received.

"How so?"

"You make over fifty-five per cent."

"Indeed!"

"Yes—look at it. You have just paid one hundred and sixty dollars for what will yield you two hundred and six dollars in six months,—for you must remember that you will get legal interest on the claim you have bought. Now this is a fraction over fifty-five per cent. per annum. What do you think of that for an investment?"

"Capital! But have you much of this kind of business?"

"Enough to, keep several thousand dollars constantly employed for you."

"Good!"

With this brief ejaculation, that came from Wolford's heart, he turned away and left the office.

On this operation, the magistrate made six per cent. The regular selling price of judgments was twenty-five per cent., with a commission of one per cent. for effecting the sale.

In a few months, Wolford had all his money invested in judgments. This business he continued for several years, meeting with but few losses. He could then write himself worth twenty-five thousand dollars, and began to find it necessary to seek for some heavier investments than buying judgments, even if they did not pay quite so well.

Loaning money on mortgages of real estate, at about ten per centum, he found a very safe business; with this he united the shaving of undoubted paper, at from one to two per cent. a month. Mr. Tompkins he had frequently shaved so closely as almost to make the blood come. This was previous to the loan before alluded to. Since that had been made, Mr. Tompkins rarely found it necessary to put good paper into Wolford's hands for discount. This the miser considered a dead loss, and he therefore determined that the loan should be taken up, and made in some quarter not likely to affect the shaving operations.

The declaration of Mr. Tompkins, that he could easily get some one else to take the mortgage, was not too well relished by Wolford, If he were sure this could be done, he would be content to accept an increase of interest and continue the loan, for the security was of the very safest kind, and ample.

"I must think about this," said he to himself, as he walked homeward, after parting with Tompkins. "I rarely make false moves, and should not like to do so in this case."

CHAPTER II.

WHEN Mr. and Mrs. Tompkins met, at dinnertime, neither of them appeared in the most happy frame of mind. The lady looked especially disagreeable. The meal passed in silence, and was eaten with little appetite.

As soon as her husband had retired from the house, which he did very soon after he had left the table, Mrs. Tompkins's manner changed.

"Humph!" said she, tossing her head, "he needn't begin the sulky game with me. Two can play at that, as he ought to know very well. I've set my heart on having a handsomer establishment than the purse-proud Mrs. Gileston, and, what is more, I will be gratified. Mr. Tompkins is worth two dollars to her husband's one, and yet she sweeps about the street with the air of a duchess, and never so much as looks me in the face, though I have been twice introduced to her. But, I'll be even with my lady! I've set my heart on this, and will move heaven and earth to accomplish it."

This half-spoken soliloquy will afford the reader some clue to the character of Mrs. Tompkins. Her husband, to whom she had been married about ten years, had gradually risen from the position of a clerk to that of a merchant, in a small way, when the death of a distant relative put him in possession of about, thirty thousand dollars. Up to that time, his wife, who was a poor girl when he married her, had been content to live in a style suited to their means. But the moment a fortune so large in her eyes, fell to their share, her ideas expanded, and she suddenly became aware of the fact that she was a woman of no mean importance.

To Mr. Tompkins, this money came just in time to save him from failure. He had started, as too many do, without capital, and had unwisely attempted to do more business than means so limited would bear. He, consequently, knew the value of money far better than his wife, and was disposed to invest what he did not require in his business, in a safe way. She, on the contrary, proposed that they should, at once, adopt a style of living in consonance with their bettered fortunes.

"We live very comfortably, as we now are," he said, in answer to a repetition of her plea for a handsome house, on the evening following the day of his interview with Wolford. "We live as well as our means have, until within a few years, enabled us to live."

Mrs. Tompkins rejoined—

"With improved fortunes, we should adopt a different style."

"I don't think we should be in any particular hurry about it," said the husband. "Let the change, if any be made, come gradually."

"All eyes are upon us," was Mrs. Tompkins's answer to this. "And everybody expects us to take a different and higher place in society."

"It is my opinion," said the husband, "that we are free to live in any style that may suit us."

"It is all very well to say that, Mr. Tompkins, but it will not do. We must, while in the world, do as the world does. People in our circumstances do not live in a rented house;—we should have a dwelling of our own, and that a handsome one—handsomer than Gileston's house, about which there, is so much talk."

"Gileston's house!" said Mr. Tompkins, in surprise. "Why that house didn't cost a cent less than twenty-five thousand dollars."

"Well, suppose it did not. What then?"

"Do you imagine that we can build a house at an expense of twenty-five thousand dollars?"

"Why not, Mr. Tompkins?"

"Where is the money to come from?"

"There it is again! But I can tell you."

"I wish to my heart you would, for it's more than I can."

"Take it out of bank, where it lies rusting."

"Humph!"

"What's the matter?"

"How much do you suppose I have in bank tonight?"

"Dear knows! Forty or fifty thousand dollars, I suppose."

"Just seventy-nine dollars and ten cents! And what is more, I have two thousand dollars to pay to-morrow, five hundred on the day after, and ten or twelve thousand more to make up within the next two weeks. If You will tell me where all this money is to come from, I will build you a dozen houses: as it is, you must build your own castles—in the air."

A flood of tears answered this bitterly spoken reply. Her tears, the lady had found, on more occasions than one, to have a powerful effect upon her husband. It must be said for her, that she did not believe a word of what Mr. Tompkins had alleged in regard to the balance of his bank account. For a man who had been in a good business for a number of years, and had received a legacy of thirty thousand dollars, to be so near out of cash, was to her mind preposterous. She knew he had invested nearly twenty thousand dollars in property, but what of that? Her tears disturbed Mr. Tompkins, as they always did.

"What I tell you is the truth, the whole truth, and nothing but the truth," said he, in a calm, but serious voice, after, the sobs of his wife had begun to die away. "And now, what would you have me do?"

"You can do just as you please, Mr. Tompkins. It is nothing to me. You know your own business best." This was said with an offended air, in which was something of indifference.

"You are unreasonable, Ellen."

"Very likely I am; at least in your eyes. I believe you never had a very exalted opinion of your wife's good sense: nor much regard for her wishes!"

"I believe, Ellen," returned the husband, "that few men regard the happiness of their wives more than I have regarded the happiness of mine. Perhaps if I had been less considerate, it might have been better for all."

"Considerate, indeed! Oh, yes! You're very considerate to buy old warehouses to rent, in place of a decent dwelling for your family! Very considerate that—wasn't it?"

At this point of the contest, Mr. Tompkins retired from the field, his forces reduced and in disorder. He saw but one hope of peace, and that was by an early surrender, and on the best terms that could be made. The property that he had purchased yielded him about fourteen hundred a year. To sell this, and build, with the proceeds, a splendid mansion, from which no income could possibly arise, seemed to him an act of egregious folly. But any thing for peace. To sell it, and put the money in his business, was a much more desirable act, instead of borrowing money, at an exorbitant interest, in order to make his payments. He had more than once thought of doing this. At the time the investment was made, his business operations were light, and he did not need the use of over ten thousand dollars of the timely legacy he had received. Since then his business had increased, and with this increase came the need of more ready money than he could command. He did not like the idea of selling his real estate, because he was very confident, from the many improvements going on in the quarter of the city where it was situated, that it would double in value in the course of ten years. He was so confident of this, that he preferred paying a high rate of interest for money for temporary purposes, rather than sell his property. So hard did he become pressed at last, that he resorted to the expedient of raising ten thousand dollars on mortgage, at ten per centum per annum. Wolford held this mortgage, as the reader is aware.

It was with painful reluctance that Mr. Tompkins made up his mind to part with his warehouse property, in order to gratify the love of display which was the besetting sin of his better half. But, even should he do that, he would have to let ten thousand dollars go to clear off the mortgage; and if it brought him twenty-two or three thousand, or even twenty-five thousand, he would not have enough to build the elegant mansion his wife desired: and should he build one in a style not consonant with her exalted ideas, his position, instead of being better, would be much worse.

The next week, to poor Mr. Tompkins, he was called a rich man, was one of sad perplexity and anxious deliberation upon what it was best for him to do. He had great difficulty in raising sufficient money to meet his payments, independent of the ten thousand dollars demanded by Wolford. Where that sum was to come from he could not tell. He had made several applications for a loan to take the place of the one now upon his property, and had even caused advertisements to be inserted in the newspapers, addressed to "capitalists," but without effect.

During all this time, Mrs. Tompkins was as disagreeable as it was possible for her to be. When her husband returned home, in the evening, sick at heart with the toil and anxiety of the day, he was met by no pleasant words or cheerful smiles. A sober face presided at his table, where the words were few and coldly spoken.

The period for which Wolford's loan had been made was within two days of its expiration, when, half beside himself with perplexity, Mr. Tompkins advertised his property for sale. There were enough who understood its real value precisely, and were ready to come forward and offer to purchase. As soon as the miser and usurer saw the course events were taking, he very kindly informed Mr. Tompkins that he had just received, unexpectedly, a large sum of money, and should not want the ten thousand dollars due him.

"You are too late," replied Mr. Tompkins, when he communicated this intelligence.

"Why so?" asked Wolford.

"I have made up my mind to sell."

"I don't want my money."

"Oh, very well, I can keep it."

"On what security."

"My note of hand."

The miser shrugged his shoulders.

"Don't you like that security?"

"I have no objection to your warehouse property."

"But that I shall sell."

Wolford retired in a dissatisfied mood. He had overreached himself.

In the course of a week the sale was made, and for cash. The property brought twenty-five thousand dollars. After the mortgage was released, and his borrowed money account balanced, Mr. Tompkins had just twelve thousand dollars to his credit in bank, with a month's heavy payments before him.

On this basis, and with this position of affairs to sustain him, Mr. Tompkins, feeling in a desperate mood, determined that he would build himself an elegant residence. The plan was furnished by an architect, and the work commenced forthwith. Mrs. Tompkins was all her husband could wish, from the day she was apprized of his decision in regard to a matter that had so long been near her heart. He said nothing of the sacrifice he had made, nor intimated any thing about what might be the ultimate consequence, although every sober thought of the future awoke a fear. The house, when finished, cost twenty-three thousand dollars; and when furnished twenty-eight thousand. It need not be said that Mr. Tompkins was hard run for money. On the day he moved into his splendid mansion, he borrowed from Mr Wolford, on a mortgage of his new property, fifteen thousand dollars, at twelve per cent. per annum. He had but one or two alternatives—to borrow at this ruinous rate of interest, or fail. The operation was for one year, without any privilege of renewal; this was the longest time at which the usurer ever loaned his money.

For one year Mrs. John Tompkins was in her glory. She gave six large parties during that time, at a heavy cost. Her husband, notwithstanding the loan of fifteen thousand dollars, was in trouble about money matters; Business had been unusually dull both in the spring and fall, and money hard to collect. Nearly ten thousand dollars, which he had fully expected to receive from distant customers, failed to come in. As the period for which he had borrowed from Wolford drew toward its close, he could not but feel uneasy. From no other quarter had he any hope of raising so large a sum as fifteen thousand dollars upon his house. He was poring over his bill-book, one day, when the man he had thought of far more frequently than was pleasant to him, came in. Mr. Tompkins felt uneasy.

"Ah—how do you do, Mr. Wolford?" said he, affecting a pleased air. "Sit down."

Wolford looked grave. He had come on business, and to him business matters were of serious import. He returned the merchant's salutation with formality, seated himself deliberately, and, resting his hands upon the head of his cane, looked up with a sinister expression on his face.

"A fine day this, Mr. Wolford," said Tompkins.

"Yes, very fine. How is business?"

"Dull—terribly dull. I have never known such a business season. There is absolutely nothing doing."

Wolford made no reply.

"I suppose you have plenty of money to lend," remarked the merchant, hardly knowing why he said so.

"No—not a dollar. It's tight with me as well as it is with you. And this brings me to the subject-matter of my visit. You are no doubt aware that, according to the terms of the loan, you are to return my fifteen thousand dollars in a few days?"

"Yes, I am aware of it. Must you have it all?"

"Every dollar; and I want three times as much, if I can get it."

"I was in hope you would renew the loan, Mr. Wolford."

"That's impossible."

"I really don't see how I am to raise fifteen thousand dollars in a few days—these times."

"You have had long enough to make it up, I am sure. You knew very well that the loan would come due next week, and that it was only for one year."

"Yes, I knew all that, very well."

"And yet you are not prepared to pay it?"

"No, I certainly am not to-day. What I may be in a week is more than I can tell."

Wolford did not want the money he had loaned to Mr. Tompkins—that is, he had no use for it. But he could never rest contented for any length of time under the reflection that another person was enjoying his money. He took an insane delight, too, in making others feel his power. If Mr. Tompkins had obtained the amount, and tendered it to Wolford, two weeks before it was due, the miser would have, in all probability, solicited him to keep it on even better terms than at first obtained; but to appear anxious about the matter, was to foreclose all chances of a renewal.

CHAPTER III.

AFTER Wolford had left the store of Mr. Tompkins, the merchant tried to rally his thoughts, and review the whole matter calmly. Thinking, however, did not make him feel much better. He could not see his way clear. If the loan were not paid off, his property would, he had not the least doubt, be sold forthwith, under the mortgage.

"I was a fool ever to build such a house, and involve myself as I have done," he murmured, fretfully. "I wish to my heart it was in the bottom of the sea. Between my wife's extravagance and this accursed usurer, I shall be ruined at last."

This was uttered almost involuntarily, but it had the effect to give his thoughts a new direction. After thinking intensely for some time, he took a long inspiration, compressed his lips tightly as he breathed out again, and then said, half aloud, and in a tone of decision—

"I will not suffer myself to be made a fool of any longer, by wife or usurer. Mrs. John Tompkins will have to lay aside a portion of her dignity, or get some other means of supporting it. I am called a man, and I will be a man."

On the evening of that day, while seated at the tea-table, Mrs. Tompkins said—

"Have you ever noticed, dear, the beautiful equipage of Mrs. Van D——?"

"The what?"

"The beautiful establishment of Mrs. Van D——?"

"What kind of an establishment?"

The manner of her husband disturbed the self-satisfaction of Mrs. Tompkins. Her reply was not in so bland a voice.

"Her carriage and pair, I mean, of course."

"No; I never notice such things."

"You don't, indeed!"

"No."

"Don't you ever expect to keep a carriage?"

"I do not."

"I am sure you will."

"You labour under a mistake, Ellen. I have no such intention."

"If I wish for one, I am sure you will gratify me." Mrs. Tompkins spoke softly and smiled.

"No—not even to gratify you, Ellen." Mr. Tompkins spoke seriously, and his brow contracted.

"You built this beautiful house to gratify me."

"True—and by doing so have set myself half crazy."

"Mr. Tompkins, I don't understand you. You are in a strange mood this evening."

"And so would you be in a strange mood, if you had suffered as much as I have during the day."

"Suffered! What have you suffered about?"

"Because I built this house."

"You speak in riddles. Why do you not explain yourself?" Mrs. Tompkins's voice trembled, and there were tears in her eyes.

"I will explain myself, Ellen," said her husband, his manner becoming serious and earnest: it had been fretful and captious before. "I was weak enough to yield to your urgent desire to have an elegant mansion, as you called it, and build this house, at a very heavy cost. I knew that I was doing wrong at the time, and that both you and I would live to regret the act of folly. But you held the reins, and I suffered myself to be driven. The consequence is, that I am involved in difficulties, and this house has to be sold within ten days."

Mr. Tompkins paused. He wished to see the effect of what he had said. Had an earthquake shaken the house to its foundation, Mrs. Tompkins could not have been more astonished than she was by this speech. Her face became deadly pale; she trembled violently from head to foot, and panted like a frightened hare. To utter a word in reply was impossible. The husband was startled at the effect produced, but did not waver an instant in his purpose. The suddenness of the annunciation had one good effect: it opened the eyes of Mrs. Tompkins completely. The manner of her husband left no doubt upon her mind that all he had said was true—that the house would have to go, spite of all he could do to save it. He might be to blame for getting into difficulties—might have mismanaged his business—but that could not alter the present position of things. On recovering from the shock occasioned by so astounding a declaration, she did not resort to any of her old tricks to manage her husband. She felt that they would be useless. As soon as she could speak, she said, firmly—

"Is all this true?"

"As true as you live and breathe."

"And it is my fault?"

"I am sorry that I cannot say otherwise." There was a good deal of feeling in the husband's tone as he made this reply. "I need not relate how I strove to convince you that I could not afford to build such a house—that to sell my warehouse property, in order to do so, would be to rob myself of at least seven or eight thousand dollars—for that property would inevitably increase in value this amount in the next five years. Already it has been sold at an advance of three thousand dollars on what I received for it. I need not relate how unhappy you made both yourself and me, until I consented to do as you wished. It is all within your remembrance. A man cannot stand every thing. I had trouble enough, even then, with my business—but found no compensation at home. In a desperate mood, I resolved to make home pleasant, if possible. I made the sacrifice, and here is the result!"

Mrs. Tompkins wept bitterly when her husband ceased speaking. Every word went to her heart. She saw her folly, nay, her crime, in having acted as she had done. She was a weak, vain woman, but not all perverted. Notwithstanding rank weeds had long overgrown the garden of her mind, some plants of goodly promise yet remained.

On the next day, without hesitating a moment, Mr. Tompkins went to a real-estate broker, and employed him to sell his house as quickly as possible. He mentioned this to his wife, as a thing of course, and suggested the necessity of disposing of their splendid furniture, and retiring from their too prominent position in the social world.

"There is but one way of safety and peace," he said, "and that way we must take, whether the entrance to it be smooth or thorny."

"Why need we sell our handsome furniture?" asked Mrs. Tompkins, in a hoarse voice.

"For the same reason that we have for selling our house," firmly returned her husband—"because it is necessary."

Mr. Tompkins spoke so decidedly, that his wife felt that remonstrance would be unavailing. Having once admitted the truth of all he had alleged, she had no ground for opposition. Completely subdued, she became altogether passive, and left her husband to do just as he pleased. The pressing nature of his affairs made him prompt to carry out all the reforms he had proposed. In less than a week he found a purchaser for his house, and was able to sell it on tolerably fair terms. The real-estate agent who had made the sale for him, had left his store but a short time after communicating all the preliminaries of the transaction, when old Wolford entered with a slow gait and a look of resolution.

"Will you be ready with that money to-morrow?" said he, fixing his small, keen eyes upon the merchant, and bending his brows.

"No!" was the decisive answer.

"Then I shall foreclose the mortgage."

"You will not do that, certainly," returned Tompkins, in a quiet tone, something like a smile playing about his lips.

"Won't I? Don't trust to that, my friend. I always keep contracts to the letter, and exact them from others, when made to me, as rigidly. You borrowed my money for a year, on a mortgage of your property. That year is up to-morrow. If the money does not come, I will immediately have your property sold."

"I have been ahead of you," coolly replied Tompkins.

"What do you mean?"

"I have already sold the property."

The miser seemed stunned by the intelligence.

"Sold it?" he asked, after a moment—"why have you sold it?"

"In order to get out of your clutches, now and for ever. You have had a good deal of my money in your time, and fool enough have I been to let you get your fingers upon it! But you will never get another dollar from me! You were not content with eighteen hundred dollars a year as the interest on fifteen thousand—wasn't I a fool to pay it?—but you must try to put your foot still more heavily on my neck! But you have overreached yourself. Your mortgage on my property is not worth that!—(snapping his fingers.) Didn't you know this before?"

"What do you mean?" Wolford showed considerable alarm.

"You took twelve per cent. per annum?"

"I know I did."

"And that is usury?"

"It is a fair interest. Money is always worth the market price."

"The law says that all over six per cent. is usury; and the taking of such excess vitiates the transaction."

"Do you mean to put in that plea?"

"Yes, if you take the first step toward foreclosing your mortgage, or show yourself in my store until I send for you, which I will do when it is perfectly convenient for me to pay your fifteen thousand dollars, and not before."

"Oh, take your time, Mr. Tompkins—take your time—I am in no particular hurry for the money," said Wolford, with an altered tone and manner—"Just when it is convenient will suit me."

"Are you sure of that?" said the merchant, speaking with a slight sneer upon his lip.

"Oh, yes! I thought I would need the money now, but I believe I will not. The mortgage can remain as long as you want it."

"I don't want it long," muttered Tompkins, turning toward his desk, and taking no further notice of the alarmed and discomfited usurer.

In about two weeks he had the pleasure of handing him the whole amount of the loan, and getting a release of the property. Wolford tried to be very affable and apologetic; but he was treated according to the merchant's estimation of his real character, and not otherwise.

"Free from your clutches, and for ever!" said Mr. Tompkins, speaking to himself, as he stepped into the street from Wolford's dwelling, feeling lighter in heart than he had felt for a long time. "What madness, with the means I have had in my hands, ever to have fed your avaricious maw!"

Although Mr. Tompkins could see the sky by looking upward, he was still in the forest, and had a hard journey before him, ere he gained the pleasant champaign he was seeking so eagerly. The cash he received on selling his house was barely sufficient to clear it of all encumbrance. He was, therefore, still hard pressed for money in his business. The sale of his handsome furniture would help him a good deal, and he determined, resolutely, to have this done forthwith. His wife ventured a demurrer, which he immediately overruled. She had lost the ability to contend with him. A sale at auction was proposed.

"Just think of the exposure," urged his wife.

"I don't care a fig for that. A protested note would be a worse exposure. I must have the money. We can board for a couple or three years, or keep house in a plain way, until I make up some of the losses sustained by our folly."

Mrs. Tompkins was passive. A vendue was called, and three thousand dollars in cash realized. This succour came just in time, for it saved the merchant's credit, and met his pressing demands, until he could turn the paper given in part payment for his house, into money. From that time he began to feel his business resting less heavily upon his shoulders. Money came in about as fast as he needed it. In a few months he began to have quite a respectable balance in bank—a thing he had not known for years.

It was a good while before Mrs. Tompkins could hold up her head in society, where she had, for some time, held it remarkably high. She never carried it as stately as before. As for Wolford, he but seldom passed the store of the merchant: when he did so, it was not without a pang—he had lost a good customer by grinding him too hard, and could not forgive himself for the error.

THE TWO INVALIDS.

THE chamber in which the sick woman lay was furnished with every thing that taste could desire or comfort demand. Yet, from none of these elegant surroundings came there an opiate for the weary spirit, or a balm to soothe the pain from which she suffered. With heavy eyes, contracted brow, and face almost as white as the lace-fringed pillow it pressed, canopied with rich curtains, she reclined, sighing away the weary hours, or giving, voice to her discontent in fruitless complainings.

She was alone. A little while before, her attendant had left the room, taking with her a child, whose glad spirits—glad because admitted to his mother's presence—had disturbed her.

"Take him out," she had said, fretfully.

"You must go back to the nursery, dear." The attendant spoke kindly, as she stooped to lift the child in her arms.

"No—no—no. I want to stay here. Do let me stay here, won't you?"

"Mamma is sick, and you disturb her," was answered.

"Oh no. I won't disturb her. I'll be so good."

"Why don't you take him out at once?" exclaimed the mother, in a harsh, excited voice. "It's too much that I can't have a little quiet! He's made my head ache already. What does nurse mean by letting him come over here?"

As the screaming child was borne from the room, the sick woman clasped her hand to her temples, murmuring—

"My poor head! It was almost quiet; but now it throbs as if every vein were ready to burst! Why don't they soothe that child?"

But the child screamed on, and his voice came ringing upon her ears. Nurse was cross, and took no pains to hush his cries; so the mother's special attendant remained, for some time, away from the sick-chamber. By slow degrees she succeeded in diverting the child's mind from his disappointment; but it was many minutes after his crying ceased before he would consent to her leaving him.

In the mean time the sun's bright rays had found a small opening in one of the curtains that draped the windows, and commenced pouring in a few pencils of light, which fell, in a bright spot, on a picture that hung against the wall; resting, in fact upon the fair forehead of a beautiful maiden, and giving a hue of life to the features. It was like a bit of fairy-work—a touch almost of enchantment. The eyes of the invalid were resting on this picture as the magic change began to take place.

How the lovely vision, if it might so be called, won her from thoughts of pain! Ah, if we could say so? Raising herself, she grasped the pendent tassel of the bell-rope, and rang with a violent hand; then sank down with a groan, exhausted by the effort, shut her eyes, and buried her face in the pillow. Leaving the only half-comforted child, her attendant hastily obeyed the summons.

"The sun is blinding me!" said the unhappy invalid, as she entered the chamber. "How could you be so careless in arranging the curtains!"

A touch, and the sweet vision which had smiled all so vainly for the poor sufferer, was lost in shadows. There was a subdued light, and almost pulseless silence in the chamber.

"Do take those flowers away, their odour is dreadful to me!"

A beautiful bouquet of sweet flowers, sent by a sympathizing friend, was removed from the chamber. Half an hour afterward—the attendant thought her sleeping—she exclaimed—

"Oh, how that does worry me!"

"What worries you, ma'am?" was kindly asked.

"That doll on the mantel. It is entirely out of place here. I wish you would remove it. Oh, dear, dear! And that toilette-glass—straighten it, if you please. I can't bear any thing crooked. And there's Mary's rigolette on the bureau; the careless child! She never puts any thing away."

These little annoyances were removed, and the invalid was quiet again—externally quiet, but within all was fretfulness and mental pain.

"There come the children from school," she said, as the ringing of the door-bell and gay voices were heard below. "You must keep them from my room. I feel unusually nervous to-day, and my head aches badly."

Yet, even while she spoke, two little girls came bounding into the room, crying—

"Oh, mother! Dear mother! We've got something good to tell you. Miss Martin says we've been two of the best"——

The attendant's imperative "H-u-s-h!" and the mother's hand waving toward the door, the motion enforced by a frowning brow, were successful in silencing the pleased and excited children, who, without being permitted to tell the good news they had brought from school, and which they had fondly believed would prove so pleasant to their mother's ears, were almost pushed from the chamber.

No matter of surprise is it that a quick revulsion took place in their feelings. If the voice of wrangling reached, soon after, the mother's ears, and pained her to the very soul, it lessened not the pressure on her feelings to think that a little self-denial on her part, a little forgetfulness of her own feelings, and a thoughtfulness for them, would have prevented unhappy discord.

And so the day passed; and when evening brought her husband to her bedside, his kind inquiries were answered only by complainings—complainings that made, from mental reactions, bodily suffering the greater. For so long a time had this state of things existed that her husband was fast losing his wonted cheerfulness of temper. He was in no way indifferent to his wife's condition; few men, in fact, could have sympathized more deeply, or sought with more untiring assiduity to lighten the burden which ill-health had laid upon her. But, in her case, thought was all turned to self. It was like the blood flowing back in congestion upon the heart, instead of diffusing itself healthfully over the system.

Thus it went on—the invalid growing worse instead of better. Not a want was expressed that money did not supply; not a caprice or fancy or appetite, which met not a proffered gratification. But all availed not. Her worst disease was mental, having its origin in inordinate selfishness. It never came into her mind to deny herself for the sake of others; to stifle her complaints lest they should pain the ears of her husband, children, or friends; to bear the weight of suffering laid upon her with at least an effort at cheerfulness. And so she became a burden to those who loved her. In her presence the sweet voices of children were hushed, and smiles faded away. Nothing that was gay, or glad, or cheerful came near her that it did not instantly change into sobriety or sadness.

Not very far away from the beautiful home of this unhappy invalid, is another sufferer from ill-health. We will look in upon her. The chamber is poorly furnished, containing scarcely an article the absence of which would not have abridged the comfort of its occupant. We enter.

What a light has come into those sunken eyes, and over that pale face! We take the thin, white hand; a touch of sadness is in our voice that will not be repressed, as we make inquiries about her health; but she answers cheerfully and hopefully.

"Do you suffer pain?"

"Yes; but mostly at night. All day long I find so much to interest me, and so many thoughts about my children fill my mind, that I hardly find time to think of my own feelings. Care is a blessing."

With what a patient, heavenly smile this is said! How much of life's true philosophy is contained in that closing sentence! Yes, care is a blessing. What countless thousands would, but for daily care, be unutterably miserable. And yet we are ever trying to throw off care; to rise into positions where we will be free from action or duty.

The voice of a child is now heard. It is crying.

"Dear little Aggy! What can ail her?" says the mother, tenderly. And she inclines an ear, listening earnestly. The crying continues.

"Poor child! Something is wrong with her. Won't you open the door a moment?"

The door is opened, and the sick mother calls the name of "Aggy" two or three times. But her voice too feeble to reach the distant apartment.

We second the mother's wishes, and go for the grieving little one.

"Mother wants Aggy."

What magic words! The crying has ceased instantly, and rainbow smiles are seen through falling tears.

"Dear little dove! What has troubled it?" How tender and soothing and full of love is the voice that utters these words! We lift Aggy upon the bed. A moment, and her fresh warm cheek is close to the pale face of her mother; while her hand is nestling in her bosom.

The smile that plays so beautifully over the invalid's face has already answered the question we were about to ask—"Will not the child disturb you?" But our face has betrayed our thoughts, and she says—

"I can't bear to have Aggy away from me. She rarely annoys me. A dear, good child—yet only a child, for whom only a mother can think wisely. She rarely leaves my room that she doesn't get into some trouble; but my presence quickly restores the sunshine."

The bell rings. There is a murmur of voices below; and now light feet come tripping up the stairs. The door opens and two little girls enter, just from school. Does the sick mother put up her hand to enjoin silence? Does she repel them,—by look or word? Oh no.

"Well, Mary—well, Anna?" she says, kindly. They bend over and kiss her gently and lovingly; then speak modestly to the visitor.

"How do you feel, mother?" asks the oldest of the two girls. "Does your head ache?"

"Not now, dear. It ached a little while ago; but it is better now."

"What made it ache, mother?"

"Something troubled Aggy, and her crying sent a pain through my temples. But it went away with the clouds that passed from her darling little face."

"Why, she's asleep, mother!" exclaimed Anna.

"So she is. Dear little lamb! Asleep with a tear on her cheek. Turn her crib around, love, so that I can lay her in it."

"No, you mustn't lift her," says Mary. "It will make your head ache." And the elder of the children lifts her baby-sister in her arms, and carefully lays her in the crib.

"Did you say all your lessons correctly this morning?" now asks the mother.

"I didn't miss a word," answers Mary.

"Nor I," says Anna.

"I'm glad of it. It always does me good to know that you have said your lessons well. Now go and take a run in the yard for exercise."

The little girls leave the chamber, and soon their happy voices came ringing up from the yard. The sound is loud, the children in their merry mood unconscious of the noise they make.

"This is too loud. It will make your head ache," we say, making a motion to rise, as if going to check the exuberance of their spirits.

"Oh no," is answered with a smile. "The happy voices of my children never disturb me. Were it the sound of wrangling, my weak head would throb instantly with pain. But this comes to me like music. They have been confined for hours in school, and health needs a reaction. Every buoyant laugh or glad exclamation expands their lungs, quickens the blood in their veins, and gives a measure of health to mind as well as body. The knowledge of this brings to me a sense of pleasure; and it is better for me, therefore, that they should be gay and noisy for a time, after coming out of school, than it would be if they sat down quietly in the house, or moved about stealthily, speaking to each other in low tones lest I should be disturbed."

We could not say nay to this. It was true, because unselfish, philosophy.

"Doesn't that hammering annoy you?" we ask.

"What hammering?"

"In the new building over the way."

She listens a moment, and then answers—

"Oh no. I did not remark it until you spoke. Such things never disturb me, for the reason that my mind is usually too much occupied to think of them. Though an invalid, and so weak that my hands are almost useless, I never let my thoughts lie idle. A mother, with three children, has enough to occupy her mind usefully—and useful thoughts, you know, are antidotes to brooding melancholy, and not unfrequently to bodily pain. If I were to give way to weaknesses—and I am not without temptations—I would soon be an unhappy, nervous, helpless creature, a burden to myself and all around me."

"You need sympathy and strength from others," we remark.

"And I receive it in full measure," is instantly replied. "Not because I demand it. It comes, the heart-offering of true affection. Poorly would I repay my husband, children, and friends, for the thousand kindnesses I receive at their hands, by making home the gloomiest place on all the earth. Would it be any the brighter for me that I threw clouds over their spirits? Would they more truly sympathize with me, because I was for ever pouring complaints into their ears? Oh no. I try to make them forget that I suffer, and, in their forgetfulness, I often find a sweet oblivion. I love them all too well to wish them a moment's sadness."

What a beautiful glow was on her pale countenance as she thus spoke!

We turn from the home of this cheerful invalid with a lesson in our hearts not soon to be forgotten. Ill-health need not always bring gloom to our dwellings. Suffering need not always bend the thoughts painfully to self. The body may waste, the hands fall nerveless to the side, yet the heart retain its greenness, and the mind its power to bless.

MARRYING WELL.

"AND so, dear," said Mrs. Waring to her beautiful niece, Fanny Lovering, "you are about becoming a bride." The aunt spoke tenderly, and with a manner that instantly broke down all barriers of reserve.

"And a happy bride, I trust," returned the blushing girl, as she laid her hand in that of her aunt, and leaned upon her confidingly.

"Pray heaven it may be so, Fanny." Mrs. Waring's manner was slightly serious. "Marriage is a very important step; and in taking it the smallest error may become the fruitful source of unhappiness."

"I shall make no error, Aunt Mary," cried the lovely girl. "Edward Allen is one of the best of young men; and he loves me as purely and tenderly as any maiden could wish to be loved. Oh, I want you to see him so much!"

"I will have that pleasure soon, no doubt."

"Yes, very soon. He is here almost every evening."

"Your father, I understand, thinks very highly of him."

"Oh yes. He is quite a pet of father's," replied Fanny.

"He's in business, then, I suppose?"

"Yes. He keeps a fancy dry-goods' store, and is doing exceedingly well—so he says."

Mrs. Waring sat silent for some time, lost in a train of reflection suddenly started in her mind.

"You look serious, aunt. What are you thinking about?" said Fanny, a slight shadow flitting over her countenance.

Mrs. Waring smiled, as she answered—

"People at my age are easily led into serious thoughts. Indeed, I can never contemplate the marriage of a young girl like yourself, without the intrusion of such thoughts into my mind. I have seen many bright skies bending smilingly over young hearts on the morning of their married life, that long ere noon were draped in clouds."

"Don't talk so, dear aunt!" said the fair young girl. "I know that life, to all, comes in shadow as well as sunshine. But, while the sky is bright, why dim its brightness by thoughts of the time when it will be overcast. Is that true philosophy, Aunt Mary?"

"If such forethought will prevent the cloud, or provide a shelter ere the storm breaks, it may be called true philosophy. But, forgive me, dear, for thus throwing a shadow where no shadow ought to rest. I will believe your choice a wise one, and that a happy future awaits you."

"You cannot help believing this when you see Edward. He will be here to-night; then you will be able to estimate him truly."

As Fanny had said, the young man called in after tea, when Mrs. Waring was introduced. Allen responded to the introduction somewhat coldly. In fact he was too much interested in Fanny herself to think much, or care much for the stranger, even though named as a relative. But, though he noticed but casually, and passed only a few words with Mrs. Waring, that lady was observing him closely, and noting every phase of character that was presented for observation; and, ere he left her presence, had read him far deeper than he imagined.

"And now, Aunt Mary, tell me what you think of Edward," said Fanny Lovering, as soon as the young man had departed, and she was alone with Mrs. Waring.

"I must see him two or three times more ere I can make up my mind in regard to him," said Mrs. Waring with something evasive in her manner. "First impressions are not always to be relied on," she added, smiling.

"Ah! I understand you,"—Fanny spoke with a sudden gayety of manner —"you only wish to tease me a little. Now, confess at once, dear Aunt Mary, that you are charmed with Edward."

"I am not much given to quick prepossessions," answered Mrs. Waring. "It may be a defect in my character; but so it is. Mr. Allen, no doubt, is a most excellent young man. You are sure that you love him, Fanny?"

"Oh, Aunt Mary! How can you ask such a question? Are we not soon to be married?"

"True. And this being so, you certainly should love him. Now, can you tell me why you love him?"

"Why, aunt!"

"My question seems, no doubt, a strange one, Fanny. Yet, strange as it may appear to you, it is far from being lightly made. Calm your mind into reflection, and ask yourself, firmly and seriously, why you love Edward Allen. True love ever has an appreciating regard for moral excellence—and knowledge must precede appreciation. What do you know of the moral wisdom of this young man, into whose hands you are about placing the destinies of your being for time—it may be for eternity? Again let me put the question—Why do you love Edward Allen?"

Fanny looked bewildered. No searching interrogations like these had been addressed to her, even by her parents; and their effect was to throw her whole mind into painful confusion.

"I love him for his excellent qualities, and because he loves me," she at length said, yet with a kind of uncertain manner, as if the reply did not spring from a clear mental perception.

"What do you mean by excellent qualities?" further inquired Mrs. Waring.

Tears came into Fanny's sweet blue eyes, as she answered—

"A young girl like me, dear Aunt Mary, cannot penetrate very deeply into a man's character. We have neither the opportunity nor the experience upon which, coldly, to base an accurate judgment. The heart is our guide. In my own case its instincts, I am sure, have not betrayed me into a false estimate of my lover. I know him to be good and noble; and I am sure his tender regard for the maiden he has asked to become his bride, will ever lead him to seek her happiness, as she will seek his. Do not doubt him, aunt."

Yet, Mrs. Waring could not help doubting him. The young man had not impressed her favourably. No word had fallen from his lips during the evening unmarked by her—nor had a single act escaped observation. In vain had she looked, in his declarations of sentiments, for high moral purposes—for something elevated and manly in tone. In their place she found only exceeding worldliness, or the flippant commonplace.

"No basis there, I fear, on which to build," said Mrs. Waring, thoughtfully, after parting with her niece for the night. "Dear, loving, confiding child! The heart of a maiden is not always her best guide. Like the conscience, it needs to be instructed; must be furnished with tests of quality."

On the day following, Mrs. Waring went out alone. Without, seeming to have any purpose in her mind, she had asked the number of Mr. Allen's store, whither she went with the design of making a few purchases. As she had hoped it would be, the young man did not recognise her as the aunt of his betrothed. Among the articles, she wished to obtain was a silk dress. Several pieces of goods were shown to her, one of which suited exactly, both in colour and quality.

"What is the price of this?" she asked.

The answer was not prompt. First, the ticket-mark was consulted; then came a thoughtful pause; and then the young storekeeper said—

"I cannot afford to sell you this piece of goods for less than a dollar thirteen."

"A dollar thirty, did you say?" asked Mrs. Waring, examining the silk more closely.

"Ye—yes, ma'am," quickly replied Allen. "A dollar thirty. And it's a bargain at that, I do assure you."

Mrs. Waring raised her eyes and looked steadily for a moment or two into the young man's face.

"A dollar and thirty cents," she repeated.

"Yes, ma'am. A dollar thirty," was the now assured answer. "How many yards shall I measure off for you?"

"I want about twelve yards."

"There isn't a cheaper piece of goods in market," said the young man, as he put his scissors into the silk—"not a cheaper piece, I do assure you. I had a large stock of these silks at the opening of the season, and sold two-thirds of them at a dollar and a half. But, as they are nearly closed out, I am selling the remainder at a trifle above cost. Can I show you any thing else, ma'am?"

"Not to-day, I believe," replied Mrs. Waring, as she took out her purse. "How much does it come to?"

"Twelve yards at one dollar and thirty cents—just fifteen dollars and sixty cents," said Allen.

Mrs. Waring counted out the money, and, as she handed it to the young man, fixed her eyes again searchingly upon him.

"Shall I send it home for you?" he asked.

"No—I will take it myself," said Mrs. Waring, coldly.

"What have you been buying, aunt?" inquired Fanny, when Mrs. Waring had returned home with her purchase.

"A silk dress. And I want to know what you think of my bargain?"

The silk was opened, and Fanny and her mother examined and admired it.

"What did you pay for it, sister?" asked Mrs. Lovering, the mother of Fanny.

"A dollar and thirty cents," was answered.

"Not a dollar thirty?" Marked surprise was indicated.

"Yes. Don't you think it cheap?"

"Cheap!" said Fanny. "It isn't worth over a dollar at the outside. Mr. Allen has been selling the same goods at ninety and ninety-five."

"You must certainly be in error," replied Mrs. Waring.

"Not at all," was the positive assertion. "Where did you get the silk?"

A somewhat indefinite answer was given; to which Fanny returned—

"I only wish we had known your intention. Mother would have gone with you to Edward's store. It is too bad that you should have been so cheated. The person who sold you the silk is no better than downright swindler."

"If it is as you say," replied Mrs. Waring, calmly, "he is not an honest man. He saw that I was a stranger, ignorant of current prices, and he took advantage of the fact to do me a wrong. I am more grieved for his sake than my own. To me, he loss is only a few dollars; to him—alas! by what rule can we make the estimate?"

Much more was said, not needful here to repeat. In the evening, Edward Allen called to see Fanny, who spoke of the purchase made by Mrs. Waring. Her aunt was present. The silk was produced in evidence of the fact that she had been most shamefully wronged by some storekeeper.

"For what can you sell goods of a similar quality?" was the direct question of Fanny.

The moment Allen saw the piece of silk, he recognised it as the same he had sold in the morning. Turning quickly, and with a flushing countenance, to that part of the room where Mrs. Waring sat, partly in the shadow, he became at once conscious of the fact that she was the purchaser. The eyes of Fanny followed those of the lover, and then came back to his face. She saw the o'ermantling blush; the sudden loss of self-possession, the quailing of his glance beneath the fixed look of Mrs. Waring. At once the whole truth flashed upon her mind, and starting up, she said, in a blended voice of grief and indignation—

"Surely, surely, Edward, you are not the man!"

Before Allen could reply, Mrs. Waring said firmly: "Yes, it is too true. He is the man!"

At this, Fanny grew deadly pale, staggered toward her mother, and sunk, sobbing wildly, upon her bosom.

Too much excited and confused for coherent explanation, and too clearly conscious of his mean dishonesty toward a stranger, Allen attempted no vindication nor excuse, lest matters should assume even a worse aspect. A moment or two he stood irresolute, and then retired from the house. As he did so, Mr. Lovering entered the room where this little scene had just transpired, and was quite startled at the aspect of affairs.

"What's this? What has happened? Fanny, child, what in the name of wonder is the matter? Where's Edward?"

Mr. Lovering spoke hurriedly. As soon as practicable, the whole affair was related.

"And is that all?" exclaimed Mr. Lovering, in surprise. "Pooh! pooh! I'm really astonished! I thought that some dreadful thing had happened."

"Don't you regard this as a very serious matter?" inquired Mrs. Waring.

"Serious? No! It's a thing of every day occurrence. If you are not a judge of the goods you attempt to purchase, you must expect to pay for your ignorance. Shopkeepers have to make up their ratio of profits in the aggregate sales of the day. Sometimes they have to sell a sharp customer at cost, rather than lose the sale; and this must be made up on some one like you."

"Not a serious matter," replied Fanny's aunt, "to discover that the betrothed of your daughter is a dishonest man?"

"Nonsense! nonsense! you don't know what you are talking about," said Mr. Lovering, fretfully. "He's shrewd and sharp, as every business-man who expects to succeed must be. As to his trade operations, Fanny has nothing to do with them. He'll make her a kind husband, and provide for her handsomely. What more can she ask?"

"A great deal more," replied Mrs. Waring, firmly.

"What more, pray?"

"A husband, in whose high moral virtues, and unselfish regard for the right, she can unerringly confide. One who will never, in his eager desire to secure for himself some personal end or gratification, forget what is due to the tender, confiding wife who has placed all that is dear to her in his guardianship. Brother, depend upon it, the man who deliberately wrongs another to gain an advantage to himself, will never, in marriage, make a truly virtuous woman happy. This I speak thoughtfully and solemnly; and I pray you take it to heart, ere conviction of what I assert comes upon you too late. But, I may have said too much. Forgive my plain speaking. From the fulness of the heart is this utterance."

And so saying, Mrs. Waring passed from the room, and left the parents of Fanny alone with their weeping child. Few words were spoken by either Mr. or Mrs. Lovering. Something in the last remarks of Mrs. Waring had startled their minds into new convictions. As for the daughter, she soon retired to her own apartment, and did not join the family again until the next morning. Then, her sad eyes and colorless face too plainly evidenced a night of sleeplessness and suffering.

By a kind of tacit consent on the part of each member of the family, no allusion, whatever, was made to the occurrences of the day previous. Evening came, but not as usual came Edward Allen. The next day, and the next went by, without his accustomed appearance. For a whole week his visits were omitted.

Grievous was the change which, in that time, had become visible in Fanny Lovering. The very light of her life seemed to go out suddenly; and, for a while, she had groped about in thick darkness. A few feeble rays were again becoming visible; but from a quarter of the heavens where she had not expected light. Wisely, gently, and unobtrusively had Mrs. Waring, during this period of gloom and distress, cast high truths into the mind of her suffering niece—and from these, as stars in the firmament of thought, came the rays by which she was able to see a path opening before her. When, at the end of the tenth day of uncertainty, came a note from Allen, in these brief words: "If it is Miss Lovering's wish to be free from her engagement, a word will annul the contract"—she replied, within ten minutes, "Let the contract be annulled; you are free."

Two weeks later, and Mr. Lovering brought home the intelligence that Allen was to be married in a few days to a certain Miss Jerrold, daughter of a man reputed wealthy.

"To Miss Jerrold! It cannot be!" said Mrs. Lovering in surprise.

"I will not believe it, father." Fanny spoke with quivering lips and a choking voice.

"Who is Miss Jerrold?" asked Mrs. Waring.

"A coarse, vulgar-minded girl, of whom many light things have been said," replied Mrs. Lovering, indignantly. "But her father is rich, and she is an only child."

"He never loved you, dear," said Mrs. Waring to Fanny about a week later, as the yet suffering girl laid her tearful face on her bosom. The news had just come that Miss Jerrold was the bride of Allen. The frame of the girl thrilled for a moment or two; then all was calm, and she replied—

"Not as I wished to be loved. O aunt! what an escape I have made! I look down the fearful gulf on the very brink of which my feet were arrested, and shudder to the heart's core. If he could take her, he never could have appreciated me. Something more than maiden purity and virtue attracted him. Ah! how could my instincts have been so at fault!"

"Dear child," said Mrs. Waring, earnestly, "there can be no true love, as I have before said to you, without an appreciation of quality. A fine person, agreeable manners, social position—in a word, all external advantages and attractions are nothing, unless virtue be in the heart. It is a man's virtues that a woman must love, if she loves truly. If she assumes the possession of moral wisdom, without undoubting evidence, she is false to herself. To marry under such circumstances is to take a fearful risk. Alas! how many have repented through a long life of wretchedness. Can a true woman love a man who lacks principle —who will sacrifice honour for a few paltry dollars—who will debase himself for gain—whose gross sensuality suffocates all high, spiritual love? No! no! It is impossible! And she who unites herself with such a man, must either shrink, grovelling, down to his mean level, or be inconceivably wretched."

Two years later, and results amply justified the timely interposition of Mrs. Waring, and demonstrated the truth of her positions. Her beautiful, true-hearted niece has become the bride of a man possessing all the external advantages sought to be obtained by Mr. and Mrs. Lovering in the proposed marriage with Mr. Allen; and what is more and better, of one whose love of truth and goodness is genuine, and whose appreciation of his wife rests on a perception of her womanly virtues. As years pass, and their knowledge of each other becomes more intimate, their union will become closer and closer, until affection and thought become so blended, that they will act in all their mutual life-relations as one.

Alas! how different it is already with Edward Allen and the woman he led to the altar, where each made false vows the one to the other. There were no qualities to be loved; and to each, person and principles soon grew repellant. Through sharp practices in business, Allen is rapidly adding to the fortune already acquired by trade and marriage; but, apart from the love of accumulation, which keeps his mind active and excited during business hours, he has no pleasure in life. He does not love the woman who presides in his elegant home, and she affects nothing in regard to him. They only tolerate each other for appearance sake. Sometimes, Fanny Lovering, now Mrs. ——, meets them in public; but never without an almost audibly breathed "Thank God, that I am not in her place!" as her eyes rest upon the countenance of Allen, in which evil and selfish purposes have already stamped their unmistakable meanings.

BLESSING OF A GOOD DEED.

"I SHOULD like to do that, every day, for a year to come," said Mr. William Everett, rubbing his hands together quickly, in irrepressible pleasure.

Mr. Everett was a stock and money broker, and had just made an "operation," by which a clear gain of two thousand dollars was secured. He was alone in his office: or, so much alone as not to feel restrained by the presence of another. And yet, a pair of dark, sad eyes were fixed intently upon his self-satisfied countenance, with an expression, had he observed it, that would, at least, have excited a moment's wonder. The owner of this pair of eyes was a slender, rather poorly dressed lad, in his thirteenth year, whom Mr. Everett had engaged, a short time previously, to attend in his office and run upon errands. He was the son of a widowed mother, now in greatly reduced circumstances. His father had been an early friend of Mr. Everett. It was this fact which led to the boy's introduction into the broker's office.

"Two thousand dollars!" The broker had uttered aloud his satisfaction; but now he communed with himself silently. "Two thousand dollars! A nice little sum that for a single day's work. I wonder what Mr. Jenkins will say tomorrow morning, when he hears of such an advance in these securities?"

From some cause, this mental reference to Mr. Jenkins did not increase our friend's state of exhilaration. Most probably, there was something in the transaction by which he had gained so handsome a sum of money, that, in calmer moments, would not bear too close a scrutiny—something that Mr. Everett would hardly like to have blazoned forth to the world. Be this as it may, a more sober mood, in time, succeeded, and although the broker was richer by two thousand dollars than when he arose in the morning, he was certainly no happier.

An hour afterward, a business friend came into the office of Mr. Everett and said—

"Have you heard about Cassen?"

"No; what of him?"

"He's said to be off to California with twenty thousand dollars in his pockets more than justly belongs to him."

"What!"

"Too true, I believe. His name is in the list of passengers who left New York in the steamer yesterday."

"The scoundrel!" exclaimed Mr. Everett, who, by this time, was very considerably excited.

"He owes you, does he?" said the friend.

"I lent him three hundred dollars only day before yesterday."

"A clear swindle."

"Yes, it is. Oh, if I could only get my hands on him!".

Mr. Everett's countenance, as he said this, did not wear a very amiable expression.

"Don't get excited about it," said the other. "I think he has let you off quite reasonably. Was that sum all he asked to borrow?"

"Yes."

"I know two at least, who are poorer by a couple of thousands by his absence."

But Mr. Everett was excited. For half an hour after the individual left who had communicated this unpleasant piece of news, the broker walked the floor of his office with compressed lips, a lowering brow, and most unhappy feelings. The two thousand dollars gain in no way balanced in his mind the three hundred lost. The pleasure created by the one had not penetrated deep enough to escape obliteration by the other.

Of all this, the boy with the dark eyes had taken quick cognizance. And he comprehended all. Scarcely a moment had his glance been removed from the countenance or form of Mr. Everett, while the latter walked with uneasy steps the floor of his office.

As the afternoon waned, the broker's mind grew calmer. The first excitement produced by the loss, passed away; but it left a sense of depression and disappointment that completely shadowed his feelings.

Intent as had been the lad's observation of his employer during all this time, it is a little remarkable that Mr. Everett had not once been conscious of the fact that the boy's eyes were steadily upon him. In fact he had been, as was usually the case too much absorbed in things concerning himself to notice what was peculiar to another, unless the peculiarity were one readily used to his own advantage.

"John," said Mr. Everett, turning suddenly to the boy, and encountering his large, earnest eyes, "take this note around to Mr. Legrand."

John sprang to do his bidding; received the note and was off with unusual fleetness. But the door which closed upon his form did not shut out the expression of his sober face and humid glance from the vision of Mr. Everett. In fact, from some cause, tears had sprung to the eyes of the musing boy at the very moment he was called upon to render a service; and, quicker than usual though his motions were, he had failed to conceal them.

A new train of thought now entered the broker's mind. This child of his old friend had been taken into his office from a kind of charitable feeling—though of very low vitality. He paid him a couple of dollars a week, and thought little more, about him or his widowed mother. He had too many important interests of his own at stake, to have his mind turned aside for a trifling matter like this. But now, as the image of that sad face—for it was unusually sad at the moment when Mr. Everett looked suddenly toward the boy—lingered in his mind, growing every moment more distinct, and more touchingly beautiful, many considerations of duty and humanity were excited. He remembered his old friend, and the pleasant hours they had spent together in years long since passed, ere generous feelings had hardened into ice, or given place to all-pervading selfishness. He remembered, too, the beautiful girl his friend had married, and how proudly that friend presented her to their little world as his bride. The lad had her large, dark, spiritual eyes—only the light of joy had faded therefrom, giving place to a strange sadness.

All this was now present to the mind of Mr. Everett, and though he tried once or twice during the boy's absence to obliterate these recollections, he was unable to do so.

"How is your mother, John?" kindly asked the broker, when the lad returned from his errand.

The question was so unexpected, that it confused him.

"She's well—thank you, sir. No—not very well, either—thank you, sir."

And the boy's face flushed, and his eyes suffused.

"Not very well, you say?" Mr. Everett spoke with kindness, and in a tone of interest. "Not sick, I hope?"

"No, sir; not very sick. But"——

"But what, John," said Mr., Everett, encouragingly.

"She's in trouble," half stammered the boy, while the colour deepened on his face.

"Ah, indeed? I'm sorry for that. What is the trouble, John?"

The tears which John had been vainly striving to repress now gushed over his face, and, with a boyish shame for the weakness, he turned away and struggled for a time with his overmastering feelings. Mr. Everett was no little moved by so unexpected an exhibition. He waited with a new-born consideration for the boy, not unmingled with respect, until a measure of calmness was restored.

"John," he then said, "if your mother is in trouble, it may be in my power to relieve her."

"O sir!" exclaimed the lad eagerly, coming up to Mr. Everett, and, in the forgetfulness of the moment, laying his small hand upon that of his employer, "if you will, you can."

Hard indeed would have been the heart that could have withstood the appealing, eyes lifted by John Levering to the face of Mr. Everett. But Mr. Everett had not a hard heart. Love of self and the world had encrusted it with indifference toward others, but the crust was now broken through.

"Speak freely, my good lad," said he, kindly. "Tell me of your mother. What is her trouble?"

"We are very poor, sir." Tremulous and mournful was the boy's voice. "And mother isn't well. She does all she can; and my wages help a little. But there are three of us children; and I am the oldest. None of the rest can earn any thing. Mother couldn't help getting behind with the rent, sir, because she hadn't the money to pay it with. This morning, the man who owns the house where we live came for some money, and when mother told him that she had none, he got, oh, so angry! and frightened us all. He said, if the rent wasn't paid by to-morrow, he'd turn us all into the street. Poor mother! She went to bed sick."

"How much does your mother owe the man?" asked Mr. Everett.

"Oh, it's a great deal, sir. I'm afraid she'll never be able to pay it; and I don't know what we'll do."

"How much?"

"Fourteen dollars, sir," answered the lad.

"Is that all?" And Mr. Everett thrust his hand into his pocket. "Here are twenty dollars. Run home to your mother, and give them to her with my compliments."

The boy grasped the money eagerly, and, as he did so, in an irrepressible burst of gratitude, kissed the hand from which he received it. He did not speak, for strong emotion choked all utterance; but Mr. Everett saw his heart in his large, wet eyes, and it was overflowing with thankfulness.

"Stay a moment," said the broker, as John Levering was about passing through the door. "Perhaps I had better write a note to your mother."

"I wish you would, sir," answered the boy, as he came slowly back.

A brief note was written, in which Mr. Everett not only offered present aid, but promised, for the sake of old recollections that now were crowding fast upon his mind, to be the widow's future friend.

For half an hour after the lad departed, the broker sat musing, with his eyes upon the floor. His thoughts were clear, and his feelings tranquil. He had made, on that day, the sum of two thousand dollars by a single transaction, but the thought of this large accession to his worldly goods did not give him a tithe of the pleasure he derived from the bestowal of twenty dollars. He thought, too, of the three hundred dollars he had lost by a misplaced confidence; yet, even as the shadow cast from that event began to fall upon his heart, the bright face of John Levering was conjured up by fancy, and all was sunny again.

Mr. Everett went home to his family on that evening, a cheerful-minded man. Why? Not because he was richer by nearly two thousand dollars. That circumstance would have possessed no power to lift him above the shadowed, fretful state which he loss of three hundred dollars had produced. Why? He had bestowed of his abundance, and thus made suffering hearts glad; and the consciousness of this pervaded his bosom with a warming sense of delight.

Thus it is, that true benevolence carries with it, ever a double blessing. Thus it is, that in giving, more is often gained than in eager accumulation or selfish withholding.

PAYING THE DOCTOR.

AFTER a day of unusual anxiety and fatigue, Dr. Elton found himself snugly wrapped up in a liberal quantity of blankets and bed-quilts, just as the clock struck twelve one stormy night in February. For over half an hour he had lain awake, racking his brain in reference to two or three critical cases which were on his hands; but tired nature could keep up no longer, and the sweet oblivion of sleep was stealing over his senses. But just as he had lost himself, the bell over his head began to ring furiously, and brought him into the middle of the floor in an instant. Pushing his head out of the window, he interrogated the messenger below, just too late to save that individual the trouble of giving the bell-rope another violent demonstration of his skill.

"Mr. Marvel wants you to come and see Charley immediately," replied the messenger.

"What's the matter with Charley?"

"He's got the croup, I believe."

"Tell him I'll be there in a moment," said Dr. Elton, drawing in his head. Hurrying on his clothes, he descended to his office, and, possessing himself of some necessary medicines, it being too late for the family to send out a prescription, wrapped his cloak around him, and turned out into the storm.

It was at least half a mile to the residence of Mr. Marvel, and by, the time the doctor arrived there, he was cold, wet, and uncomfortable both in mind and body. Ascending to the chamber, he was not a little surprised to find Charley, a bright little fellow of some two years old, sitting up in his crib as lively as a cricket.

"O doctor! we've been so frightened!" said Mrs. Marvel, as Dr. Elton entered. "We thought Charley had the croup, he breathed so loud. But he don't seem to get any worse. What do you think of him, doctor?"

Dr. Elton felt his pulse, listened to his respiration, examined the appearance of his skin, and then said, emphatically—

"I think you'd better all be in bed!"

"It's better to be scared than hurt, doctor," responded Mr. Marvel.

"Humph!" ejaculated Dr. Elton.

"Don't you think you'd better give him something, doctor?" said Mrs. Marvel.

"What for, ma'am?"

"To keep him from having the croup. Don't you think he's threatened with it?"

"Not half as much as I am," replied the doctor, who made a quick retreat, fearing that he would give way too much to his irritated feelings, and offend a family who were able to pay.

Next morning, on the debtor side of his ledger, under the name of Mr. Marvel, Dr. Elton made this entry; To one night-visit to son,$5. "And it's well for me that he's able to pay," added the doctor, mentally, as he replaced the book in the drawer from which he had taken it. Scarcely had this necessary part of the business been performed, when the same messenger who had summoned him the night before, came post-haste into the office, with the announcement that Mrs. Marvel wanted him to come there immediately, as Charley had got a high fever.

Obedient to the summons, Dr. Elton soon made his appearance, and found both Mr. and Mrs. Marvel greatly concerned about their little boy.

"I'm so 'fraid of the scarlet fever, doctor!" said Mrs. Marvel. "Do you think it's any thing like that?" she continued with much anxiety, turning upon Charley a look of deep maternal affection.

Dr. Elton felt of Charley's pulse, and looked at his tongue, and then wrote a prescription in silence.

"What do you think of him, doctor?" asked the father, much concerned.

"He's not dangerous, sir. Give him this, and if he should grow worse, send for me."

The doctor bowed and departed, and the fond parents sent off for the medicine. It was in the form of a very small dose of rhubarb, and poor Charley had to have his nose held tight, and the nauseous stuff poured down his throat. In the afternoon, when the doctor called, on being sent for, there were some slight febrile symptoms, consequent upon excitement and loss of rest. The medicine, contrary to his expectation, heightened, instead of allaying these; and long before nightfall he was summoned again to attend his little patient. Much to his surprise, he found him with a hot skin, flushed face, and quickened pulse. Mrs. Marvel was in a state of terrible alarm.

"I knew there was more the matter with him than you thought for, doctor!" said the mother, while Dr. Elton examined his patient. "You thought it was nothing, but I knew better. If you'd only prescribed last night, as I wanted you to, all this might have been saved."

"Don't be alarmed, madam," said the doctor, "there is nothing serious in this fever. It will soon subside."

Mrs. Marvel shook her head.

"It's the scarlet fever, doctor, I know it is!" said she, passionately, bursting into tears.

"Let me beg of you, madam, not to distress yourself. I assure you there is no danger!"

"So you said last night, doctor; and just see how much worse he is getting!"

As Dr. Elton was generally a man of few words, he said no more, but wrote a prescription, and went away, promising, however, at the earnest request of Mrs. Marvel, to call again that night.

About nine o'clock he called in, and found Charley's fever in no degree abated. Mrs. Marvel was in tears, and her husband pacing the floor in a state of great uneasiness.

"O doctor, he'll die, I'm sure he'll die!" said Mrs. Marvel, weeping bitterly.

"Don't be alarmed, my dear madam," replied the doctor. "I assure you it is nothing serious."

"Oh, I'm 'sure it's the scarlet fever! It's all about now."

"No, madam, I am in earnest when I tell you it is nothing of the kind. His throat is not in the least sore."

"Yes, doctor, it is sore!"

"How do you know?" responded the doctor, examining Charley's mouth and throat, which showed not the least symptom of any irritation of the mucous membrane. "It can't be sore from any serious cause. Some trifling swelling of the glands is all that can occasion it, if any exist."

Thus assured, and in a positive manner, Mrs. Marvel's alarm in some degree abated, and after ordering a warm bath, the doctor retired.

About three o'clock the doctor was again sent for in great haste. On entering the chamber of his little patient, he found his fever all gone, and he in a pleasant sleep.

"What do you think of him, doctor?" asked Mrs. Marvel, in a low, anxious whisper.

"I think he's doing as well as he can."

"But a'n't it strange, doctor, that he should breathe so low? He looks so pale, and lays so quiet! Are you sure he's not dying?"

"Dying!" exclaimed Dr. Elton,—"he's no more dying than you are! Really, Mrs. Marvel, yon torment yourself with unnecessary fears! Nature is only a little exhausted from struggling with the fever, he will be like a new person by morning."

"Do not mistake the case, doctor, for we are very much concerned," said Mr. Marvel.

"I do assure you, sir, that I understand the case precisely; and you must believe me, when I tell you that no patient was ever in a better way than your little boy."

Next morning, among other charges made by Dr. Elton, were two against Mr. Marvel, as follows: To four visits to son, $4. To one night-visit to son, $5.

"Not a bad customer!" said the doctor, with a smile, as he ran up the whole account, and then closed the book.

In the constant habit of sending for the doctor on every trifling occasion, whether it occurred at noonday or midnight, it is not to be wondered at that a pretty large bill should find its way to Mr. Marvel at the end of the year. And this was not the worst of it; the health of his whole family suffered in no slight degree from the fact of each individual being so frequently under the influence of medicine. Poor Charley was victimized almost every week; and, instead of being a fresh, hearty boy, began to show a pale, thin face, and every indication of a weakened vital action. This appearance only increased the evil, for both parents, growing more anxious in consequence, were more urgent to have him placed under treatment. Dr. Elton sometimes remonstrated with them, but to no purpose; and yielding to their ignorance and their anxiety, became a party in the destruction of the boy's health.

"What is that, my dear?" asked Mrs. Marvel of her husband, some ten months after their introduction to the reader, as the latter regarded, with no pleasant countenance, a small piece of paper which he held in his hand.

"Why, it's Dr. Elton's bill."

"Indeed! How much is it?"

"One hundred and fifty dollars!"

"Oh, husband!"

"Did you ever hear of such a thing?"

"One hundred and fifty dollars, did you say?"

"Yes, one hundred and fifty dollars. A'n't it outrageous?"

"It's scandalous! It's downright swindling! I'd never pay it in the world! Who ever heard of such a thing! One hundred and fifty dollars for one year's attendance! Good gracious!"—and Mrs. Marvel held up her hands, and lifted her eyes in profound astonishment.

"I can't understand it!" said Mr. Marvel. "Why, nobody's had a spell of sickness in the family for the whole year. Charley's been a little sick once or twice; but nothing of much consequence. There must be something wrong about it. I'll go right off and see him, and have an understanding about it at once."

Carrying out his resolution on the instant, Mr. Marvel left the house and proceeded with rapid steps toward the office of Dr. Elton. He found that individual in.

"Good morning Mr. Marvel! How do you do to-day?" said the doctor, who understood from his countenance that something was wrong, and had an instinctive perception of its nature.

"Good morning, doctor! I got your bill to-day."

"Yes, sir; I sent it out."

"But a'n't there something wrong about it, doctor?"

"No, I presume not. I make my charges carefully, and draw off my bills in exact accordance with them."

"But there must be, doctor. How in the world could you make a bill of one hundred and fifty dollars against me? I've had no serious sickness in my family."

"And yet, Mr. Marvel, I have been called in almost every week, and sometimes three or four times in as many days."

"Impossible!"

"I'll show you my ledger, if that will satisfy you, where every visit is entered."

"No, it's no use to do that. I know that you have been called in pretty often, but not frequently enough to make a bill like this."

"How many night-visits do you suppose I have made to your family, during the year?"

"I'm sure I don't know. Not more than three or four."

"I've made ten!"

"You must be mistaken, doctor."

"Do you remember that I was called in last February, when you thought Charley had the croup?"

"Yes."

"And the night after?"

"Yes. That's but two."

"And the night you thought he had the measles?"

"Yes."

"And the night after?"

"Yes. But that's only four."

"And the three times he fell out of bed?"

"Not three times, doctor!"

"Yes, it was three times. Don't you recollect the knob on his head?"

"Yes, indeed!"

"And the sprained finger?"

"Yes."

"And the bruised cheek?"

"Well, I believe you are right about that, doctor. But that don't make ten times."

"You have not forgotten, of course, the night he told you he had swallowed a pin?"

"No, indeed," said the father, turning pale. "Do you think there is any danger to be apprehended from its working its way into the heart, doctor?"

"None at, all, I should think. And you remember"—

"Never mind, doctor, I suppose you are right about that. But how can ten visits make one hundred and fifty dollars?"

"They will make fifty, though, and that is one-third of the bill."

"You don't pretend to charge five dollars a visit, though, doctor?"

"For all visits after ten o'clock at night, we are allowed by law to charge five dollars."

"Outrageous!"

"Would you get up out of your warm bed after midnight, turn out in a December storm, and walk half a mile for five dollars?"

"I can't say that I would. But then it's your business."

"Of course it is, and I must be paid for it."

"Any how, doctor, that don't account for the whole of this exorbitant bill."

"But one hundred day and evening visits here on my ledger will, though."

"You don't pretend to say you have paid my family a hundred visits, certainly?"

"I will give you day and date for them, if necessary."

"No, it's no use to do that," said Mr. Marvel, whose memory began to be a little more active. "I'll give you a hundred dollars, and say no more about it; that is enough, in all conscience."

"I can't do any such thing, Mr. Marvel. I have charged you what was right, and can take nothing off. What would you think of a man who had made a bill at your store of one hundred and fifty dollars, if he were to offer you one hundred when he came to pay, and ask for a receipt in full?"

"But that a'n't to the point."

"A'n't it, though? I should like to hear of a case more applicable. But it's no use to multiply words about the matter. My bill is correct, and I cannot take a dollar off of it."

"It's the last bill you ever make out of me, remember that, doctor!" said Mr. Marvel, rising, and leaving the office in a state of angry excitement.

"Well, what does he say?" asked Mrs. Marvel, who had waited for her husband's return with some interest.

"He tried to beat me down that the bill was all right; but I'm too old a child for that. Why, would you believe it?—he has charged five dollars for every night-visit."

"That's no better than highway robbery."

"Not a bit. But it's the last money he ever gets out of me."

"I'd never call him in, I know. He must think we're made of money."

"Oh, I suppose we're the first family he's had who wasn't poor, and he wanted to dig as deep as possible. I hate such swindling, and if it wasn't for having a fuss I'd never pay him a dollar."

"He's charged us for every poor family in the neighbourhood, I suppose."

"No doubt of it. I've heard of these tricks before; but it's the last time I'll submit to have them played off upon me."

The visit of Mr. Marvel somewhat discomposed the feelings of Dr. Elton, and he had begun to moralize upon the unthankful position he held in the community, when he was aroused from his reverie by the entrance of a servant from one of the principal hotels, with a summons to attend immediately a young lady who was thought to be exceedingly ill.

"Who is she?" asked the doctor.

"She is the daughter of Mr. Smith, a merchant from the East."

"Is any one with her?"

"Yes, her father."

"Tell him I will be there immediately."

In the course of fifteen minutes Dr. Elton's carriage drove up to the door of the hotel. He found his patient to be a young lady of about seventeen, accompanied by her father, a middle-aged man, whose feelings were much, and anxiously excited.

At a glance, his practised eye detected symptoms of a serious nature, and a closer examination of the case convinced him that all his skill would be called into requisition. With a hot, dry skin, slightly flushed face, parched lips, and slimy, furred tongue, there was a dejection, languor, and slight indication of delirium—and much apparent confusion of mind. Prescribing as he thought the case required, he left the room, accompanied with the father.

"Well, doctor, what do you think of her?" said Mr. Smith, with a heavy, oppressed expiration.

"She is ill, sir, and will require attention."

"But, doctor, you don't think my child dangerous, do you?" said the father with an alarmed manner.

"It is right that you should know, sir, that your daughter is, to all appearance, threatened with the typhus fever. But I don't think there is any cause for alarm, only for great care in her physician and attendants."

"O doctor, can I trust her in your hands? But I am foolish; I know that there is no one in this city of more acknowledged skill than yourself. You must pardon a father's fears. Spare no attentions, doctor—visit her at least twice every day, and you shall be well paid for your attentions. Save my child for me, and I will owe you eternal gratitude."

"All that I can do for her, shall be done, sir," said Dr. Elton.

Just relieved from the care of a dangerous case, in its healthy change, Dr. Elton's mind had relaxed from the anxiety which too frequently burdened it; for a physician's mind is always oppressed while the issue, of life or death hangs upon his power to subdue a disease, which may be too deeply seated to yield to the influence of medicine. Now, all the oppressive sense of responsibility, the care, the anxiety, were to be renewed, and felt with even a keener concern.

In the evening he called in, but there was no perceptible change, except a slight aggravation of all the symptoms. The medicine had produced no visible salutary effect. During the second day, there was exhibited little alteration, but on the morning of the third day, symptoms of a more decided character had supervened—such as suffused and injected eyes, painful deglutition, an oppression in the chest, accompanied with a short, dry cough, pains in the back, loins, and extremities; and a soreness throughout the whole body. These had not escaped the father's observation, and with the most painful anxiety did he watch the countenance of the physician while he examined the case in its new presentation. Much as he tried to control the expression of his face, he found it impossible. He felt too deeply concerned, and was too conscious of the frequent impotence of medicine, when administered with the most experienced skill.

In the afternoon he called again, and found the father, as usual, by the bedside. His patient seemed to be in a narcotic sleep, and when roused from it, complained of much giddiness, and soon sunk down again into a state of torpor.

"What do you think of her now, doctor?" asked the father, in a hoarse whisper, on the physician's leaving the chamber of his patient.

"It is impossible to form any correct idea respecting a case like this. I have seen many much worse recover, and have no doubt, as far as human calculation will go, that your daughter will get well. But the fever is a tedious one, usually defying all attempts at breaking it. It must run its course, which is usually some ten or fifteen days. All we can do is to palliate, and then assist nature, when the disease has abated its violence."

It is not necessary to trace the progress of the disease from day to day, until it reached its climax. When the fever did break, and a soft, gentle moisture penetrated the skin, the patient had but a spark of life remaining.

At the close of the fifteenth day, when every symptom indicated that convalescence or death would soon ensue, no one but a physician can imagine the painful, restless anxiety, which was felt by Dr. Elton. He took but little food, and slept hardly any during the whole night, frequently starting from his brief periods of troubled slumber, in consequence of great nervous excitement.

Early in the morning he called at the room of his patient, trembling, lest a first glance should dash every hope to the ground. He entered softly, and perceived the father bending over her with a pale anxious face. She was asleep. He took her hand, but let it drop instantly.

"What is the matter?" asked the father in an alarmed whisper, his face growing paler.

"She is safe?" responded the doctor, in a low whisper, every pulse thrilling with pleasant excitement.

The father clasped his hands, looked upward a moment, and then burst into tears.

"How can I ever repay you for your skill in saving my child!" he said, after his feelings had grown calmer.

It was nearly a month before the daughter was well enough to return home, during most of which time Dr. Elton was in attendance. For fifteen days he had attended twice a day regularly, and for nearly as long a period once a day.

While sitting in his office one day about three o'clock, waiting for his carriage to come up to the door, Mr. Smith entered, and asked for his bill, as he was about to leave. On examining his account-book, Dr. Elton found that he had made about fifty visits, and accordingly he made out his bill fifty dollars.

"How much is this, doctor?" said Mr. Smith, eyeing the bill with something of doubt in the expression of his countenance.

"Fifty dollars, sir."

"Fifty dollars! Why, surely, doctor, you are not going to take advantage of me in that way?"

"I don't understand you, sir."

"Why, I never heard of such an extravagant bill in my life. I have my whole family attended at home for fifty dollars a year, and you have not been visiting one of them much over a month."

"Such as the bill is, you will have to pay it, sir. It is just, and I shall not abate one dollar," responded Dr. Elton, considerably irritated.

Mr. Smith drew out his pocket-book slowly, selected a fifty-dollar bill from a large package, handed it to the doctor, took his receipt, and rising to his feet, said emphatically—

"I am a stranger, and you have taken advantage of me. But remember, the gains of dishonesty will never prosper!" and turning upon his heel, left the office.

"Who would be a doctor?" murmured Dr. Elton, forcing the unpleasant thoughts occasioned by the incident from his mind, and endeavouring to fix it upon a case of more than usual interest which he had been called to that day.

A word to the wise is sufficient; it is therefore needless to multiply scenes illustrative of the manner in which too many people pay the doctor.

When any one is sick, the doctor is sent for, and the family are all impatient until he arrives. If the case is a bad one, he is looked upon as a ministering angel; the patient's eye brightens when he comes, and all in the house feel more cheerful for hours after. Amid all kinds of weather, at all hours in the day or night, he obeys the summons, and brings all his skill, acquired by long study, and by much laborious practice, to bear upon the disease. But when the sick person gets well, the doctor is forgotten; and when the bill appears, complaint at its amount is almost always made; and too frequently, unless he proceed to legal measures, it is entirely withheld from him. These things ought not so to be. Of course, there are many honourable exceptions; but every physician can exclaim—"Would that their number was greater!"

THE LITTLE BOUND-BOY.

IN a miserable old house, in Commerce street, north of Pratt street Baltimore,

—there are fine stores there now—lived a shoemaker, whose wife took a particular fancy to me as a doctor, (I never felt much flattered by the preference,) and would send for me whenever she was sick. I could do no less than attend her ladyship. For a time I tried, by pretty heavy bills, to get rid of the honour; but it wouldn't do. Old Maxwell, the husband, grumbled terribly, but managed to keep out of my debt. He was the reputed master of his house; but I saw enough to satisfy me that if he were master, his wife was mistress of the master.

Maxwell had three or four apprentices, out of whom he managed to get a good deal of work at a small cost. Among these was a little fellow, whose peculiarly delicate appearance often attracted my attention. He seemed out of place among the stout, vulgar-looking boys, who stitched and hammered away from morning until night in their master's dirty shop.

"Where did you get that child?" I asked of the shoemaker one day.

"Whom do you mean? Bill?"

"Yes, the little fellow you call Bill."

"I took him out of pure charity. His mother died about a year and a half ago, and if I hadn't taken him in, he would have gone to the poor house as like as not."

"Who was his mother?"

"She was a poor woman, who sewed for the slopshops for a living—but their pay won't keep soul and body together."

"And so she died?"

"Yes, she died, and I took her child out of pure charity, as I have said."

"Is he bound to you?"

"Oh yes. I never take a boy without having him bound."

"What was his mother's name?"

"I believe they called her Mrs. Miller."

"Did you ever meet with her?"

"No: but my wife knew her very well. She was a strange kind of woman—feeling something above her condition, I should think. She was always low-spirited, my wife says, but never complained about any thing. Bill was her only child, and he used to go for her work, and carry it home when it was finished. She sent him out, too, to buy every thing. I don't believe she would have stirred beyond her own door if she had starved to death."

"Why not?"

"Pride, I reckon."

"Pride? Why should she be proud?"

"Dear knows! Maybe she once belonged to the bettermost class of people, and was afraid of meeting some of them in the street."

This brief conversation awoke an interest in my mind for the lad. As I left the shop, I met him at the door with a large bucket of water in his hand—too heavy for his strength. I looked at him more narrowly than I had ever done before. There was a feminine delicacy about every feature of his face, unusual in boys who ordinarily belong to the station he was filling. His eyes, too, had a softer expression, and his brow was broader and fairer. The intentness with which I looked at him, caused him to look at me as intently. What thoughts were awakened in his mind I could not tell. I put my hand upon his head, involuntarily; but did not speak to him; and then passed on. I could not help turning to take another glance at the boy. He had turned also. I saw that there were tears in his eyes.

"Poor fellow!" I murmured, "he is out of his place." I did, not go back to speak to him, as I wished afterward that I had done, but kept on my way.

Not having occasion to visit the shoemaker's wife again for some months, this boy did not, during the time, fall under my notice. It was midwinter when I next saw him.

I was preparing to go out one stormy morning in February, when a lad came into my office. He was drenched to the skin by the rain, that was driving fiercely along under the pressure of a strong northeaster, and shivering with cold. His teeth chattered so that it was some time before he could make known his errand. I noticed that he was clad in a much worn suit of common corduroy, the cracks in which, here and there, showed the red skin beneath, and proved clearly enough that this was all that protected him from the bitter cold. One of his shoes gaped widely at the toe; and the other was run down at the heel so badly, that part of his foot and old ragged stocking touched the floor. A common sealskin cap, with the front part nearly torn off, was in his hand. He had removed this from his head on entering, and stood, with his eyes now resting on mine, and now dropping beneath my gaze, waiting for me to ask his errand. I did not recognise him.

"Well, my little man," I said, "is any one sick?"

"Please sir, Mr. Maxwell wants you to come down and see Johnny."

"Mr. Maxwell! Do you live with Mr. Maxwell?"

"Yes, sir."

I now recognized the lad. He was a good deal changed since I last saw him, and changed for the worse.

"What is the matter with Johnny?" I asked.

"I believe he's got the croup."

"Indeed! Is he very sick?"

"Yes, sir. He can't hardly breathe at all, and goes all the time just so—" Imitating the wheezing sound attendant upon constricted respiration.

"Very well, my boy, I will be there in a little while, But, bless me! you will get the croup as well as Johnny, if you go out in such weather as this and have on no warmer clothing than covers you now. Come up to the stove and warm yourself—you are shivering all over. Why did not you bring an umbrella?"

"Mr. Maxwell never lets me take the umbreller," said the boy innocently.

"He doesn't? But he sends you out in the rain?"

"Oh yes—always. Sometimes I am wet all day."

"Doesn't it make you sick?"

"I feel bad, and ache all over sometimes after I have been wet; and sometimes my face swells up and pains me so I can't sleep."

"Do not your feet get very cold? Have you no better shoes than these?"

"I've got a better pair of shoes: but they hurt my feet so I can't wear them. Thomas, one of the boys, gave me these old ones."

"Why do they hurt your feet? Are they too small?"

"No, sir, I don't think they are. But my feet are sore."

I feared as much as this. "What is the matter with your feet?" I asked.

"I don't know, sir. The boys say that nothing's the matter with them, only they're a little snow-burnt."

"How do they feel?"

"They burn and itch, and are so tender I can hardly touch them. I can't sleep at nights sometimes for the burning and itching."

I examined the boy's feet, and found them red, shining and tumefied, with other indications of a severe attack of chilblains.

"What have you done for your feet?" I asked. "Does Mr. Maxwell know they are so bad?"

"I showed them to him, and he said it was only a snow-burn, and that I must put my feet in snow and let it draw the cold out."

"Did you do so?"

"Yes, sir, as long as I could bear it; but it hurt dreadful bad. Mr. Maxwell said I didn't keep them in half long enough."

"Were they better afterward?"

"Yes, sir, I think they were; but I go out so much in the snow, and get them wet so often, that they can't get well."

"What is your name?" I asked.

"William."

"What else?"

"William Miller."

"Is your mother alive?"

The tone and manner of the boy, when he gave a half inarticulate negative, made me regret having asked the question. It was a needless one, for already knew that his mother was dead. It was meant, however, as a preliminary inquiry, and, having been made, I proceeded to question him, in order to learn something, briefly, of his history.

"Were you born in Baltimore?" I continued.

"Yes, sir."

"Have you any relatives here?"

"Mr. P—— W—— is my uncle."

"Mr. W——?" I said, in surprise.

"Yes, sir—mother said he was my uncle."

"Is he your mother's brother?"

"Yes, sir."

"Did he ever come to see your mother?"

"No, sir, he never came near us, and mother never went to see him."

"What was the reason?"

"I don't know, sir."

The child continued to look intently in my face, but I questioned him no further. I knew Mr. W—— very well, and settled it at once in my mind that I would call and see him about the lad. I stood musing for some moments after the boy's last reply, and then said—

"Tell Mr. Maxwell, that I will call down in about half an hour: Run home as quickly as you can, and try and keep out of the rain."

The sad, rebuking earnestness with which the boy looked at me, when I said this, touched my feelings. He had, evidently, expected more than a mere expression of sympathy; but I did not think it right to create any false hopes in his mind. I meant to do all I could to relieve his wretched condition; but did not know how far I would be successful.

I found, on visiting the child of Maxwell, that I had quite a severe case of croup on my hands. His respiration was very difficult, and sounded as if the air were forced through a metallic tube. There was a good deal of fever, and other unfavourable symptoms. The albuminous secretion was large, and the formation of the false membrane so rapid as to threaten suffocation. I resorted to the usual treatment in such cases, and, happily, succeeded in producing a healthy change in the course of a few hours. So urgent had been the case, that, in attending to it, my mind had lost sight of the little boy on my first and second visits. As I was leaving the house on the morning succeeding the day on which I had been called in, I met him coming along the passage with an armful of wood. The look he gave me, as he passed, rebuked my forgetfulness, and forced me to turn back and speak to his master.

"Look here, Maxwell," I said, speaking decidedly, but in a voice so low that my words could not be heard distinctly by others in the room—"you must take better care of that boy Bill, or you will get into trouble."

"How so, doctor? I am not aware that I ill-treat him," returned the shoemaker, looking up with surprise.

"He is not clothed warmly enough for such weather as this."

"You must be mistaken. He has never complained of not feeling warm."

I took hold of Maxwell's pantaloons. They were made of coarse, thick cloth, and I perceived that there were thick woollen drawers under them.

"Take off these heavy trowsers and drawers," said I, and in place of them put on a pair of half-worn corduroy pantaloons, "and go out of doors and stand in the rain until you are drenched to the skin. The experiment will enable you to decide for yourself whether Bill is warmly enough clad."

I spoke with earnestness. Either my manner, or what I said, produced a strong effect upon the shoemaker. I could see that I had offended him, and that he was struggling to keep down a feeling of anger that was ready to pour itself forth upon me for having presumed to remark upon and interfere with his business.

"Understand me," said I, wishing to prevent the threatened outbreak of passion, "I speak as a physician, and my duty as a physician requires me to do so. The knowledge of, and the experience in diseases, which I possess, enable me to understand better than other men the causes that produce them, and to give, as I should give, to the unthinking, a warning of danger. And this I give to you now."

"All very well, doctor," returned Maxwell, "if you don't raise false alarms."

"Do you think I have done so in the present case?"

"I don't think any thing about it. I know you have."

"Then you think the lad warmly enough clothed?"

"If I did not think so, I would dress him more warmly."

"You have on three times the thickness of clothing that he has." I fixed my eyes intently on the man as I spoke.

"And his blood is three times as warm as mine. I need not tell you that, doctor."

"How do you know?"

"How do I know?" speaking contemptuously—"does not everybody know that?"

"How hot do you suppose your blood is?"

"I don't know."

"Let us suppose it to be eighty degrees. Three times eighty would be two hundred and forty. Water boils at two hundred and twelve. If it be indeed true that the lad's blood is above the boiling-point, I must agree with you that his clothes are quite sufficient to keep out the cold at any season."

"You understand me well enough, doctor," replied Maxwell, exhibiting a good deal of confusion. "I mean that a boy's blood is much warmer than a man's, which, with his greater activity, causes him to be less affected by cold. I have seen a good deal of boys, and have been a boy myself, and know all about it."

"Generally speaking, what you affirm about the greater warmth of young persons is true," I said to this. "But there are many exceptions. It is true, where there is good health, good spirits, plenty of good food, and activity. But it is not true where these are lacking. Nor is it true in any case to the extent you seem to imagine. Particularly is it not true in the case of the boy about whom we are conversing."

"Why not in his case, doctor? I can see no reason."

"He has not the vital activity of most boys of his age, and consequently not the warmth of body. His face is pale and thin, and his limbs have not the fulness of youth. He has no activity in his movements."

"Because he is a lazy fellow," replied the shoemaker, knitting his brows. "He wants the strap two or three times a day; that would make his blood circulate freely enough."

"Brutal wretch!" I could hardly keep from exclaiming. But for the boy's sake I put a curb upon my feelings.

"In doing so," I quietly replied, "you would be guilty of sad cruelty and injustice. The lad can no more help what you call laziness, than you could help being born with gray eyes. It his natural bodily temperament. He has not the robust constitution we see in most boys; and this is his misfortune, not his fault."

Maxwell replied to this by pushing out his lips, drawing up his chin, half closing his eyes, and nodding his head in a very contemptuous manner; saying almost as plainly as words could express it—"All gammon, doctor! You needn't try to come over me with that kind of nonsense."

Satisfied that it would be useless to say any thing more upon the subject at that time, I turned away, remarking as I did so—

"If you are not influenced by my advice in this matter, you may chance to feel more potent reasons. A word to the wise is sufficient."

The shoemaker made no reply, and we parted. My first impression was to go immediately to Mr. W—— and apprize him of the condition of his nephew. But a little reflection convinced me that it would be much better to make some previous inquiries in regard to his family, and endeavour to ascertain the reason of his estrangement from his sister. I would then be able to act with more certainty of success. I soon obtained all the information I desired. The history was an impressive one. I will give it as briefly as possible.

Anna W——, at the age of twenty, was esteemed and beloved by all who knew her. Her family was one of wealth and standing, and she moved in our first circles. She had but one brother, to whom she was tenderly attached. Philip was her elder by some years. Among the many who sought the regard of Anna, was a young man named Miller, who had been for years the intimate friend of her brother. Extremely fond of his sister, and highly valuing his friend for his many estimable qualities, Philip was more than gratified when he saw evidences of attachment springing up between them.

Besides Miller, Anna had another suitor, a young man named Westfield, who had become quite intimate with her, but who had made no open declaration of love before Miller came forward and offered for her hand. Westfield loved Anna passionately, but hesitated to declare his feelings, long after he had come to the conclusion that without her for his companion through life, existence would be undesirable. This arose from the fact of his not being certain in regard to the maiden's sentiments, Anna was always kind, but reserved. She was, he could see, ever pleased to meet him; but how far this pleasure was the same that she experienced in meeting other friends, he could not tell. While thus hesitating, business required him to go to New Orleans, and spend some months there. Before leaving he called three several times upon Miss W——, with the intention of making known his sentiments, but each time shrank from the avowal, and finally resolved that he would make the declaration in writing immediately on his arrival at New Orleans. With this object in view, he asked her if she were willing to correspond with him. Anna hesitated a moment or two before replying, and then assented with a blushing cheek.

For some months before this, Miller had shown more than his usual attentions to the sister of his friend; and these had been sufficiently marked to attract Anna's notice. He was a man of intelligence, fine attainments, honourable sentiments, and of good personal appearance. To his attractions the maiden was by no means insensible. But Westfield had a prior claim upon her heart— she admired the former, but loved the latter unacknowledged to herself.

Immediately on his arrival at New Orleans, Westfield wrote to Anna, but did not speak of the true nature of his feelings. The letter touched upon all subjects but the one nearest to his heart. Anna replied to it briefly, and with evident reserve. This threw such a damper upon the young man, that he did not write again for nearly two months, and then not with the warmth and freedom that had distinguished his first letter.

Meantime, Miller grew more and more constant in his attentions to Anna: To second these attentions, Philip W—— frequently alluded to his friend in terms of admiration. Gradually Anna became interested in the young man, and pleased whenever he made her a visit. When Westfield asked the privilege of opening a correspondence with her, she believed, from many corroborating circumstances, that he designed formally addressing her, and that the correspondence would lead to that result. But as his letters, with the lapse of time, grew less and less frequent, and more constrained and formal, she was led to form a different opinion. During all this time Miller's attentions increased, and Anna's feelings became more and more interested. Finally, an offer of marriage was made, and, after due reflection accepted. Three days afterward Miss W—— received the following letter:—

"NEW ORLEANS, June 8th, 18—.

"MY DEAR ANNA,

"A letter from an intimate and mutual friend prompts me at once to open to you my whole heart. For many months—nay, for more than a year—I have loved you with an ardour that has made your image ever present with me, sleeping or waking. Often and often have I resolved to declare this sentiment, but a foolish weakness has hitherto kept me silent; and now the danger of losing you constrains me to speak out as abruptly as freely. When I asked the privilege of opening a correspondence with you, it was that I might, in my very first epistle, say what I am now saying; but the same weakness and hesitation remained. Many times I wrote all I wished to say, folded and sealed the letter, and—cast it into the flames. I had not the courage to send it. Foolish weakness! I tremble to think of the consequences that may follow. Dear Anna! —I will thus address you until you forbid the tender familiarity, and bid my yearning heart despair—Dear Anna! write me at once and let me know my fate. Do not wait for a second post. Until I hear from you I shall be the most unhappy of mortals. If your heart is still free—if no promise to another has passed your lips, let me urge my suit by all the tenderest, holiest, and purest, considerations. No one can love you with a fervour and devotion surpassing mine; no heart can beat responsive to your own more surely than mine; no one can cherish you in his heart of hearts, until life shall cease, more tenderly than I will cherish you. But I will write no more. Why need I? I shall count the days and hours until your answer come.

"Yours, in life and death,

"H. WESTFIELD."

Tears gushed from the eyes of Anna W——, as she read the last line of this unlooked for epistle, her whole frame trembled, and her heart beat heavily in her bosom. It was a long time before she was sufficiently composed to answer the letter. When she did answer, it was, briefly, thus—

"BALTIMORE, June 28, 18—.

"MR. H. WESTFIELD.

"Dear Sir:—Had your letter of the 18th, come a week earlier, my answer might have been different. Now I can only bid you forget me.

"Yours, &c.

ANNA."

"Forget you?" was the answer received to this. "Forget you? Bid me forget myself! No, I can never forget you. A week!—a week earlier? Why should a single week fix our fates for ever. You are not married. That I learn from my friend. It need not, then, be too late. If you love me, as I infer from your letter, throw yourself upon the magnanimity of the man to whom you are betrothed, and he will release you from your engagement. I know him. He is generous-minded, and proud. Tell him he has not and cannot have your whole heart. That will be enough. He will bid you be free."

The reply of Anna was in these few words. "Henry Westfield; it is too late. Do not write to me again. I cannot listen to such language as you use to me without dishonour."

This half-maddened the young man. He wrote several times urging Anna by every consideration he could name to break her engagement with Miller. But she laid his letters aside unanswered.

An early day for the marriage was named. The stay of Westfield at the South was prolonged several months beyond the time at first determined upon. He returned to Baltimore a month after the proposed union of Anna with Miller had been consummated.

Although induced, from the blinding ardency of his feelings, to urge Anna to break the engagement she had formed, this did not arise from any want of regard in his mind to the sacredness of the marriage relation. So suddenly had the intelligence of her contract with Miller come upon him, coupled with the admission that if his proposal had come a week earlier it might have been accepted, that for a time his mind did not act with its usual clearness. But, when the marriage of her he so idolized took place, Westfield, as a man of high moral sense, gave up all hope, and endeavoured to banish from his heart the image of one who had been so dearly beloved. On his return to Baltimore, he did not attempt to renew his acquaintance with Anna. This he deemed imprudent, as well as wrong. But, as their circle of acquaintance was the same, and as the husband and brother of Anna were his friends, it was impossible for him long to be in the city without meeting, her. They met a few weeks after his return, at the house of a friend who had a large company. Westfield saw Anna at the opposite side of one of the parlours soon after he came in. The question of leaving the house came up and was some time debated. This he finally determined not to do, for several reasons. He could not always avoid her; and the attempt to do so would only make matters worse, for it would attract attention and occasion remarks. But, although he remained with the company, he preferred keeping as distant as possible from Anna. His feelings were yet too strong. To meet her calmly was impossible, and to meet her in any other way, would, he felt, be wrong. While he thus thought and felt, the husband of Anna touched him on the arm and said—

"Come! I must introduce you to my wife. You were one of her old friends, but have not once called upon her since your return from the South. She complains of your neglect, and, I think, justly. Come!"

Westfield could not hesitate. There was no retreat. In a space of time shorter than it takes to write this sentence, he was standing before the young bride, struggling manfully for the mastery over himself. This was only partial—not complete. Anna, on the contrary, exhibited very few, if any signs of disturbance. She received him with a warm, frank, cordial manner, that soon made him feel at ease—it caused a pleasant glow in his bosom. As soon as they had fairly entered into conversation, the young husband left them. His presence had caused Westfield to experience some restraint; this gave way as soon as he withdrew to another part of the room, and he felt that no eye but an indifferent one was upon him. An hour passed like a minute. When supper was announced, Westfield offered his arm to conduct Anna to the refreshment room. She looked around for her husband, and, not seeing him, accepted the attention. Just as they were about leaving the parlour, Miller came up, and

Westfield offered to resign his wife to his care, but he politely declined taking her from his arm. At supper, the husband and the former lover seemed to vie with each other in their attention to Anna, who never felt happier in her life. Why she experienced more pleasurable feelings than usual, she did not pause to inquire. She was conscious of being happy, and that was all.

From that time, Westfield became a regular visitor at the house of Mr. Miller, with whom he was now more intimate than before. He came and went without ceremony, and frequently spent hours with Anna while her husband was away. This intimacy continued for two or three years without attracting any attention from the social gossips who infest every circle.

"It is high time you were married."

Or—

"Westfield, why don't you go more into company?"

Or—

"I really believe you are in love with Mrs. Miller."

Were laughing remarks often made by his friends, to which he always made some laughing answer; but no one dreamed of thinking his intimacy with Anna an improper one. He was looked upon as a warm friend of both her husband and herself, and inclined to be something of an "old bachelor." If she were seen at the theatre, or on the street, with Westfield, it was looked upon almost as much a matter of course as if she were with her husband. It is but fair to state, that the fact of his ever having been an avowed lover was not known, except to a very few. He had kept his own secret, and so had the object of his misplaced affection.

No suspicion had ever crossed the generous mind of Miller, although there were times when he felt that his friend was in the way, and wished that his visits might be less frequent and shorter. But such feelings were of rare occurrence. One day, about three years after his marriage, a friend said to him, half in jest, and half in earnest—

"Miller, a'n't you jealous of Westfield?"

"Oh yes—very jealous," he returned, in mock seriousness.

"I don't think I would like my wife's old flame to be quite as intimate with her as Westfield is with your wife."

"Perhaps I would be a little jealous if I believed him to be an old flame."

"Don't you know it?"

The tone and look that accompanied this question, more than the question itself, produced an instant revulsion in Miller's feelings.

"No, I do not know it!" he replied, emphatically—"Do you know it?"

Conscious that he had gone too far, the friend hesitated, and appeared confused.

"Why have you spoken to me in the way that you have done? Are you jesting or in earnest?"

Miller's face was pale, and his lip quivered as he said this.

"Seriously, my friend," replied the other, "if you do not know that Westfield was a suitor to your wife, and only made known his love to her after you had offered her your hand, it is time that you did know it. I thought you were aware of this."

"No, I never dreamed of such a thing. Surely it cannot be true."

"I know it to be true, for I was in correspondence with Westfield, and was fully aware of his sentiments. Your marriage almost set him beside himself."

As soon as Miller could get away from the individual who gave him this startling information, he turned his steps homeward. He did not ask himself why he did so. In fact, there was no purpose in his mind. He felt wretched beyond description. The information just conveyed, awakened the most dreadful suspicions, that would not yield to any effort his generous feelings made to banish them.

On arriving at home, (it was five o'clock in the afternoon,) he found that his wife had gone out; and further learned that Westfield had called for her in a carriage, and that they had ridden out together. This information did not, in the least, tend to quiet the uneasiness he felt.

Going up into the chambers, he noticed many evidences of Anna's having dressed, herself to go out, in haste. The door of the wardrobe stood open, and also one of her drawers, with her bunch of keys lying upon the bureau. The dress she had on when he left her at dinner-time, had been changed for another, and, instead of being hung up, was thrown across a chair.

The drawer that stood open was her private drawer, in which she kept all her trinkets, and little matters particularly her own. Its contents her husband had never seen, and had never desired to see. Now, however, something more than mere curiosity prompted him to look somewhat narrowly into its contents. In one corner of this drawer he found a small casket, beautifully inlaid, that had never before come under his notice. Its workmanship was costly and exquisite. He lifted it and examined it carefully, and then taking the bunch of keys that lay before him, tried the smallest in the lock. The lid flew open. A few letters, and a small braid of hair, were its only contents. These letters were addressed to her under her maiden name. The husband was about unfolding one of them, when he let it fall suddenly into the casket, saying, as he did so—

"No, no! I have no right to read these letters. They were not addressed to my wife." With an effort he closed the drawer and forced himself from the room. But the fact that Westfield had been a suitor for the hand of Anna, and was now on terms of the closest intimacy with her, coming up vividly in his mind, he came, after some reflection, to the firm conclusion that he ought to know the contents of letters treasured so carefully—letters that he had every reason now to believe were from Westfield. Their post-mark he had noticed. They were from New Orleans.

After again hesitating and debating the question for some time, he finally determined to know their contents. He read them over and over again, each sentence almost maddening him. They were from Westfield. The reader already knows their contents. From their appearance, it was evident that they had been read over very many times; one of them bore traces of tears. For some time the feelings of Miller were in a state of wild excitement. While this continued, had his wife or Westfield appeared, he would have been tempted to commit some desperate act. But this state gradually gave way to a more sober one. The letters were replaced carefully, the casket locked, and every thing restored to its former appearance. The husband then sat down to reflect, as calmly as was in his power, upon the aspect of affairs. The more he thought, the more closely he compared the sentiments of the letters so carefully treasured with the subsequent familiarity of his wife with Westfield, the more satisfied was he that he had been deeply and irreparably wronged—wronged in a way for which there was no atonement.

As this conviction fully formed itself in his mind, the question of what he should do came up for immediate decision. He had one child, about eighteen months old, around whom his tenderest affections had entwined themselves; but when he remembered that his friend's intimacy with his wife had run almost parallel with their marriage, a harrowing suspicion crossed his mind, and made his heart turn from the form of beauty and innocence it had loved so purely.

The final conclusion of the agonized husband was to abandon his wife at once, taking with him the corroborating evidence of her unfaithfulness. He returned to her private drawer, and taking from it the letters of Westfield and the braid of hair, placed them in his pocket. He then packed his clothes and private papers in a trunk, which he ordered to be sent to Gadsby's Hotel. Half an hour, before his wife's return, he had abandoned her for ever.

When Mrs. Miller came home, it was as late as tea-time. She was accompanied by Westfield, who came into the house with his usual familiarity, intending to share with the family in their evening meal, and enjoy a social hour afterward.

Finding that her husband was not in the parlour—it was past the usual hour of his return—nor anywhere in the house, Mrs. Miller inquired if he had not been home.

"Oh yes, ma'am," said the servant to whom she spoke, "he came home more than two hours ago."

"Did he go out again?" she asked, without suspicion of any thing being wrong.

"Yes, ma'am. He went up-stairs and stayed a good while, and then came down and told Ben to take his trunk to Gadsby's."

The face of Mrs. Miller blanched in an instant. She turned quickly away and ran up to her chamber. Her drawer, which she had not noticed before, stood open. She eagerly seized her precious casket; this, too, was open, and the contents gone! Strength and consciousness remained long enough for her to reach the bed, upon which she fell, fainting.

When the life-blood once more flowed through her veins, and she was sufficiently restored to see what was passing around her, she found the servants and Westfield standing by her bedside. The latter looked anxiously into her face. She motioned him to come near. As he bent his ear low toward her face, she whispered—

"Leave me. You must never again visit this house, nor appear to be on terms of intimacy with me."

"Why?"

"Go, Mr. Westfield. Let what I have said suffice. Neither of us have acted with the prudence that should have governed our conduct, all things considered. Go at once! In time you will know enough, and more than enough."

Westfield still hesitated, but Mrs. Miller motioned him away with an imperative manner; he then withdrew, looking earnestly back at every step.

A glass of wine and water was ordered by Anna, after drinking which, she arose from the bed, and desired all her domestics to leave the room.

Meantime, her husband was suffering the most poignant anguish of mind. On retiring to a hotel, he sent for the brother of his wife, and to him submitted the letters he had taken from Anna's casket. After they had been hurriedly perused, he said—

"You know the intimacy of Westfield with Anna. Put that fact alongside of these letters and their careful preservation, and what is your conclusion?"

"Accursed villain!" exclaimed W——, grinding his teeth and stamping upon the floor, his anger completely overmastering him. "His life shall pay the price of my sister's dishonour. Madness!"

"You think, then, as I do," said the husband, with forced calmness, "that confidence, nay, every thing sacred and holy, has been violated?"

"Can I doubt? If these were his sentiments," (holding up the letters of Westfield,) "before my sister's marriage, can they have changed immediately afterward. No, no; our confidence has been basely betrayed. But the wretch shall pay for this dearly."

On the next day W—— called upon Westfield in company with a friend who had possession of the letters, and who read them as a preliminary explanation of the cause of the visit.

"Did you write those letters?" W—— asked, with a stern aspect.

"I certainly did," was the firm reply. "Do you question my right to do so?"

"No: not your right to make known to my sister your sentiments before marriage, but your right to abuse her husband's confidence after marriage."

"Who dares say that I did?"

"I dare say it," returned the brother, passionately.

"You! Bring your proof."

"I want no better proof than the fact that, entertaining sentiments such as are here avowed, you have visited her at all times, and under nearly all circumstances. You have abused a husband's and a brother's confidence. You have lain like a stinging viper in the bosom of friendship."

"It is false!" replied Westfield, emphatically.

W——'s feelings were chafed to the utmost already. This remark destroyed entirely the little self-control that remained. He sprang toward Westfield, and would have grappled his throat, had not his friend, who had feared some such result, been perfectly on his guard, and stepped between the two men in time to prevent a collision.

Nothing was now left W—— but to withdraw, with his friend. A challenge to mortal combat followed immediately. A meeting was the result, in which Westfield was severely wounded. This made public property of the whole matter; and as public feeling is generally on the side of whoever is sufferer, quite a favourable impression of the case began to prevail, grounded upon the denial of Westfield to the charge of improper intimacy with Mrs. Miller. But this feeling soon changed. The moment Mrs. Miller heard that Westfield had been seriously wounded by her brother, she flew to his bedside, and nursed him with unwearying devotion for three weeks; when he died of inflammation arising from his wound.

This act sealed her fate: it destroyed all sympathy for her; it was, in the mind of every one, proof positive of her guilt. When she returned home, the house was closed against her. An application for a divorce had already been laid before the legislature; then in session at Annapolis, and, as the inferential proofs of defection were strongly corroborated by Mrs. Miller's conduct after the hostile meeting between Westfield and her brother, the application was promptly granted, with the provision of five hundred dollars a year for her support. The decision of the legislature, with information of the annual amount settled upon her, were communicated through the attorney of her husband. Her only answer was a prompt and indignant refusal to accept the support the law had awarded her. From that moment she sank into obscurity with her child, and with her own hands earned the bread that sustained both their lives. From that moment until the day of her death, all intercourse with her family and friends was cut off. How great were her sufferings, no one can know. They must have been nearly up to the level of human endurance.

I learned this much from one who had been intimate with all the circumstances. He remembered the duel very well, but had never before understood the true cause. My informant had no knowledge whatever of Mrs. Miller from the time of her divorce up to the period of my inquiries. Miller himself still lived. I had some slight acquaintance with him.

Under this aspect of things, I hardly knew what course to pursue in order to raise the lad at Maxwell's above his present unhappy condition. I entertained, for some time, the idea of communicating with his father and uncle on the subject; but I could not make up my mind to do this. The indignation with which they had thrown off his erring mother, and the total oblivion that had been permitted to fall upon her memory, made me fearful that to approach them on the subject would accomplish no good for the boy, and might place me in a very unpleasant position toward them. Thus far I had kept my own counsel, although the nature of my inquiries about Mrs. Miller had created some curiosity in the minds of one or two, who asked me a good many questions that I did not see proper to answer directly.

"The child is innocent, even if the mother were guilty." This I said to myself very frequently, as a reason why I should make every effort in my power to create an interest in favour of little Bill, and get him out of the hands of his master, who, in my view, treated him With great cruelty. In thinking about the matter, it occurred to me that in case Mrs. Miller were innocent of the derelictions charged upon her, she would leave some evidence of the fact, for the sake of her child at least. So strongly did this idea take hold of my mind, that I determined to question Bill closely about his mother as early as I could get an opportunity. This did not occur for several weeks. I then met the boy in the street, hobbling along with difficulty. I stopped him and asked him what ailed his feet. He said they were sore, and all cracked open, and hurt him so that he could hardly walk.

"Come round to my office and let me see them," said I.

"I am going to take these shoes to the binder's,"—he had a package of "uppers" in his hand—"and must be back in twenty minutes, or Mr. Maxwell says he will give me the strap." The boy made this reply, and then hobbled on as fast as he could.

"Stop, stop, my lad," I called after him. "I want you for a little while, and will see that Mr. Maxwell does not give you the strap. You must come to my office and get something done for your feet."

"They are very bad," he said, turning round, and looking down at them with a pitiable expression on his young face.

"I know they are, and you must have something done for them immediately."

"Let me go to the binder's first."

"Very well. Go to the binder's. But be sure to come to my office as you return; I want to see you particularly."

My words made the blood rush to the child's pale face. Hope again was springing up in his bosom.

In about ten minutes he entered my office. His step was lighter, but I could see that each footfall gave him pain. The first thing I did was to examine his feet. They were in a shocking condition. One of them had cracked open in several places, and the wounds had become running sores; other parts were red and shining, and much swollen, I dressed them carefully. When I came to replace his shoes, I found them so dilapidated and out of shape, as to be no protection to his feet whatever, but rather tending to fret them, and liable to rub off the bandages I had put on. To remedy this, I sent my man out for a new pair, of soft leather. When these were put on, and he stood upon, his feet, he said that they did not hurt him at all. I needed not his declaration of the fact to convince me of this, for the whole expression of his face had changed. His eyes were no longer fixed and sad; nor were his brows drawn down, nor his lips compressed.

"I think you told me that your name was Miller?" I said to him, as he stood looking earnestly in my face after the dressing of his feet was completed.

"Yes, sir," he replied.

"And that your mother was dead?"

"Yes, sir."

"I think you said that W—— was your uncle?"

"Yes, sir. Mother told me that he was my uncle."

"Is your father living?"

"I don't know, sir."

"Did your mother ever speak to you about him?"

"No, sir."

"Then you can't tell whether he is living or not?"

"No, sir; but I suppose he is dead."

"Why do you think so?"

"Because I never saw him, nor heard mother speak of him."

"You are sure your name is Miller?"

"Oh yes, sir."

"And that Mr. W—— is your uncle?"

"My mother said he was."

"Did you ever see him?"

"No, sir."

"Why don't you go, to see him, and tell him who you are?"

"I asked mother, one day, to let me do so, but she said I must never think of such a thing."

"Why not?"

"I don't know."

"And so you never went to see him?"

"No, indeed; mother said I must not." This was said with great artlessness.

"What became of your mother's things after she died?"

"The woman we rented from took them all. Mother owed her, she said."

"Indeed! Where did you live?"

"In Commerce street, three or four doors from Mr. Maxwell's. Mother rented a room up-stairs."

"Does the woman live there still?"

"Yes, sir."

"Do you ever go to see her?"

"No, sir; she won't let me come into the house."

"Why not?"

"I cannot tell. She was going to send me to the poorhouse, when Mr. Maxwell took me in. I have often and often wanted to see the room where we lived in, and where mother died, but she wouldn't let me go up. One day I begged and cried for her to let me go up—I wanted to, so bad; but she called me a dirty little brat, and told me to go about my business, or she would get Mr. Maxwell to give me a beating. I never have tried to go there since."

"What is the woman's name?"

"Her name is Mrs. Claxon."

"And she lives three or four doors from Mr. Maxwell's?"

"Yes, sir."

"I am going home with you in a little while, and will get you to show me the house. Your mother had some furniture in her room?"

"Yes, sir. We had a bureau, and a bedstead, and a good many things."

"Do you know what was in the bureau?"

"Our clothes."

"Nothing else?"

"Mother had a beautiful little box that was always locked. It had letters in it, I think."

"Did you ever see her reading them?"

"Oh yes, often, when she thought I was asleep; and she would cry, sometimes, dreadful hard."

"This box Mrs. Claxon kept?"

"Yes, sir; she kept every thing."

"Very well. We will see if we can't make her give up some of the things."

"If she will give me that little box, she may have every thing else," said the lad.

"Why are you so desirous to have that box?"

"I sometimes think if I could get that box, and all the letters and papers it had in it, that I would be able to know better who I am, and why I mustn't go and see my uncle, who is rich, and could take me away from where I am now."

"You don't like to live with Mr. Maxwell, then?"

"Oh no, sir."

I did not question him as to the reason; that was unnecessary.

After putting up one or two prescriptions, (we had not then fallen into the modern more comfortable mode of writing them,) I told the boy that I would walk home with him, and excuse him to his master for having stayed away so long. I had no great difficulty in doing this, although the shoemaker seemed at first a little fretted at my having taken up the lad's cause again. In passing to his shop, the house where Mrs. Claxon lived was pointed out to me. Before leaving, I made Maxwell promise to let the boy come up on the next evening to get his feet dressed, telling him, what was true, that this was necessary to be done, or very serious consequences might follow.

I then called upon Mrs. Claxon. She was a virago. But the grave and important face that I put on when I asked if a Mrs. Miller did not once live in her house, subdued her. After some little hesitation, she replied in the affirmative.

"I knew as much," I said, thinking it well to let her understand from the beginning that it would not do to attempt deception.

"She died here, I believe?" I continued.

"Yes, sir; she died in my house."

"She left some property in your hands, did she not?"

"Property? Humph! If you call an old bed and bedstead, with other trumpery that didn't sell for enough to pay her back rent,property, why, then, she did leave property."

"Of course," I said, calmly. "Whatever she left was property; and, of course, in taking possession of it, you did so under a regular legal process. You took out letters of administration, I presume, and brought in your bill against the effects of the deceased, which was regularly passed by the Orphans' Court, and paid out of the amount for which the things sold."

The effect of this was just what I desired. The woman looked frightened. She had done no such thing, as I knew very well.

"If you have proceeded in this way," I resumed, "all is well enough; but if you have not done so, I am sorry to say that you will most likely get yourself into trouble."

"How so, sir?" she asked, with increasing alarm.

"The law is very rigid in all these matters. When a person dies, there must be a regular administration upon his property. The law permits no one to seize upon his effects. In the case of Mrs. Miller, if you were legally authorized to settle her estate, you can, of course, account for all that came into your hands. Now, I am about instituting a rigid examination into the matter, and if I do not get satisfaction, shall have you summoned to appear before the Orphans' Court, and answer for your conduct. Mrs. Miller was highly connected, and it is believed had papers in her possession of vital importance to the living. These were contained in a small casket of costly and curious workmanship. This casket, with its contents, must be produced. Can you produce them?"

"Y-y-yes!" the alarmed creature stammered out.

"Very well. Produce them at once, if you wish to save yourself a world of trouble."

The woman hurried off up-stairs, and presently appeared with the casket.

"It is locked," she said. "I never could find the key, and did not like to force it open. She handed me the box as she spoke.

"Yes, this is it," I remarked, as if I was perfectly familiar with the casket. "You are sure the contents have not been disturbed?"

"Oh yes: very sure."

"I trust it will be found so. I will take possession of the casket. In a few days you will hear from me."

Saying this, I arose and left the house. I directed my steps to the shop of a locksmith, whose skill quickly gave me access to the contents. They consisted mainly of papers, written in a delicate female hand; but there were no letters. Their contents were, to me, of a most gratifying kind. I read on every page the injured wife's innocence. The contents of the first paper I read, I will here transcribe. Like the others, it was a simple record of feelings, coupled with declarations of innocence. The object in view, in writing these, was not fully apparent; although the mother had evidently in mind her child, and cherished the hope that, after her death, these touching evidences of the wrong she had endured, would cause justice to be done to him.

The paper I mentioned was as follows, and appeared to have been written a short time after her divorce:—

"That I still live, is to me a wonder. But a few short months ago I was a happy wife, and my husband loved me with a tenderness that left my heart nothing to ask for. I am now cast off from his affections, driven from his home, repudiated, and the most horrible suspicions fastened upon me; And worse, the life of one who never wronged me by a look, or word, or act—in whose eyes my honour was as dear as his own—has been murdered. Oh! I shall yet go mad with anguish of spirit! There are heavy burdens to bear in this life; but none can be heavier than that which an innocent wife has to endure, when all accuse her as I am accused, and no hope of justice is left.

"Let me think calmly. Are not the proofs of my guilt strong? Those letters— those fatal letters—why did I keep them? I had no right to do so. They should have been destroyed. But I never looked at them from the day I gave my hand with my heart at the altar to one who now throws me off as a polluted wretch. But I knew they were there, and often thought of them; but to have read over one line of their contents, would have been false to my husband; and that I could not be, under any temptation. I think Westfield was wrong, under the circumstances, to visit me as constantly as he did; but my husband appeared to like his company, and even encouraged him to come. Many times he has asked him to drive me out, or to attend me to a concert or the theatre, as he knew that I wished to go, and he had business that required his attention, or felt a disinclination to leave home. In not a single instance, when I thus went out, would not my pleasure have been increased, had my husband been my companion; and yet I liked the company of Westfield—perhaps too well. The remains of former feelings may still have lingered, unknown to me, in my heart. But I was never false to my husband, even in thought; nor did Westfield ever presume to take the smallest liberty. Indeed, whether in my husband's presence, or when with me, his manner was polite, and inclined to be deferential rather than familiar. I believe that the sentiments he held toward me before my marriage, remained; and these, while they drew him to my side, made him cherish my honour and integrity as a wife, as he would cherish the apple of his eye. And yet he has been murdered, and I have been cast off, while both were innocent! Fatal haste! Fatal misjudgment! How suddenly have I fallen from the pinnacle of happiness into the dark pit of despair! Alas! alas! Who can tell what a day may bring forth?"

Another, and very important paper, which the casket contained, was a written declaration of Mrs. Miller's innocence, made by Westfield before his death. It was evidently one of his last acts, and was penned with a feeble and trembling hand. It was in these impressive words:—

"Solemnly, in the presence of God, and without the hope of living but a few hours, do I declare that Mrs. Anna Miller is innocent of the foul charges made against her by her husband and brother, and that I never, even in thought, did wrong to her honour. I was on terms of close intimacy with her, and this her husband knew and freely assented to. I confess that I had a higher regard for her than for any living woman. She imbodied all my highest conceptions of female excellence. I was never happier than when in her company. Was this a crime? It would have been had I attempted to win from her any thing beyond a sentiment of friendship. But this I never did after her marriage, and do not believe that she regarded me in any other light than as her own and her husband's friend. This is all that, as a dying man, I can do or say. May heaven right the innocent! HENRY WESTFIELD."

Besides the paper in the handwriting of Mrs. Miller, which I have given, there were many more, evidently written at various times, but all shortly after her separation from her husband. They imbodied many touching allusions to her condition, united with firm expressions of her entire innocence of the imputation under which she lay. One sentiment particularly arrested my attention, and answered the question that constantly arose in my mind, as to why she did not attempt, by means of Westfield's dying asseveration, to establish her innocence. It was this:—

"He has prejudged me guilty and cast me off without seeing me or giving me a hearing, and then insulted me by a legislative tender of five hundred dollars a year. Does he think that I would save myself, even from starvation, by means of his bounty? No—no—he does not know the woman he has wronged."

After going over the entire contents of the casket, I replaced them, and sent the whole to Mr. Miller, with a brief note, stating that they had come into my possession in rather a singular manner, and that I deemed it but right to transmit them to him. Scarcely half an hour had elapsed from the time my messenger departed, before Miller himself entered my office, pale and agitated. I had met him a few times before, and had a slight acquaintance with him.

"This is from you, I believe, doctor?" he said, holding up the note I had written him.

I bowed.

"How did you come in possession of the casket you sent me?" he continued as he took the chair I handed him.

I was about replying, when he leaned over toward me, and laying his hand upon my arm, said, eagerly—

"First tell me, is the writer of its contents living?"

"No," I replied; "she has been dead over two years."

His countenance fell, and he seemed, for some moments, as if his heart had ceased to beat. "Dead!" he muttered to himself—"dead! and I have in my hands undoubted proofs of her innocence."

The expression of his face became agonizing.

"Oh, what would I not give if she were yet alive," he continued, speaking to himself. "Dead—dead—I would rather be dead with her than living with my present consciousness."

"Doctor," said he, after a pause, speaking in a firmer voice, "let me know how those papers came into your hands?" I related, as rapidly as I could, what the reader already knows about little Bill and his mother dwelling as strongly as I could upon the suffering condition of the poor boy.

"Good heavens!" ejaculated Miller, as I closed my narrative—"can all this indeed be true? So much for hasty judgment from appearances! You have heard the melancholy history of my wife?"

I bowed an assent.

"From these evidences, that bear the force of truth, it is plain that she was innocent, though adjudged guilty of one of the most heinous offences against society. Innocent, and yet made to suffer all the penalties of guilt. Ah, sir—I thought life had already brought me its bitterest cup: but all before were sweet to the taste compared with the one I am now compelled to drink. Nothing is now left me, but to take home my child. But, as he grows up toward manhood, how can I look him in the face, and think of his mother whom I so deeply wronged."

"The events of the past, my dear sir," I urged, "cannot be altered. In a case like this, it is better to look, forward with hope, than backward with self-reproaches."

"There is little in the future to hope for," was the mournful reply to this.

"But you have a duty to perform, and, in the path of duty, always lie pleasures."

"You mean to my much wronged and suffering child. Yes, I have a duty, and it shall be performed as faithfully as lies in my power. But I hope for little from that source."

"I think you may hope for much. Your child I have questioned closely. He knows nothing of his history; does not even know that his father is alive. The only information he has received from his mother is, that W—— is his uncle."

"Are you sure of this?"

"Oh yes. I have, as I said, questioned him very closely on this point."

This seemed to relieve the mind of Mr. Miller. He mused for some minutes, and then said—

"I wish to see my son, and at once remove him from his present position. May I ask you to accompany me to the place where he now is."

"I will go with pleasure," I returned, rising.

We left my office immediately, and went direct to Maxwell's shop. As we entered, we heard most agonizing cries, mingled with hoarse angry imprecations from the shoemaker and the sound of his strap. He was whipping some one most severely. My heart misgave me that it was poor little Bill. We hurried into the shop. It was true. Maxwell had the child across his knees, and was beating him most cruelly.

"That is your son," I said, in an excited voice to Miller, pointing to the writhing subject of the shoemaker's ire. In an instant Maxwell was lying four or five feet from his bench in a corner of his shop, among the lasts and scraps of leather. A powerful blow on the side of his head, with a heavy cane, had done his. The father's hand had dealt it. Maxwell rose to his feet in a terrible fury, but the upraised cane of Miller, his dark and angry countenance, and his declaration that if he advanced a step toward him, or attempted to lay his hand again upon the boy, he would knock his brains out, cooled his ire considerably.

"Come, my boy," Miller then said, catching hold of the hand of the sobbing child—"let me take you away from this accursed den for ever."

"Stop!" cried Maxwell, coming forward at this; "you cannot take that boy away. He is bound to me by law, until he is twenty-one. Bill! don't you dare to go."

"Villain!" said Miller, in a paroxysm of anger, turning toward him—"I will have you before the the court in less than twenty-four hours for inhuman treatment of this child—of my child."

As Miller said this, the trembling boy at his side started and looked eagerly in his face.

"Oh, sir! Are you indeed my father?" said he, in a voice that thrilled me to the finger ends.

"Yes, William; I am your father, and I have come to take you home."

Tears gushed like rain over the cheeks of the poor boy. He shrank close to his father's side, and clung to him with a strong grasp, still looking up into a face that he had never hoped to see, with a most tender, confiding, hopeful, expressive countenance.

The announcement of the fact subdued the angry shoemaker. He made a feeble effort at apology, but was cut short by our turning abruptly from him and carrying of the child he had so shamefully abused.

I parted from the father and son at the first carriage-stand that came in our way. When I next saw Bill, his appearance was very different indeed from what it was when I first encountered him. His father lived some ten years from this time during the most of which period William was at school or college. At his death he left him a large property, which remained with him until his own death, which took place a few years ago. He never I believe, had the most distant idea of the cause which had separated his mother from his father. That there had been a separation he knew too well but, he always shrank from inquiring the reason, and had always remained in ignorance of the main facts here recorded.

EUTHANASY.

"YOU remember Anna May, who sewed for you about a year ago?" said one fashionably-dressed lady to another.

"That pale, quiet girl, who made up dresses for the children?"

"The one I sent you."

"Oh yes; very well. I had forgotten her name. What has become of her? If I remember rightly, I engaged her for a week or two in the fall; but she did not keep her engagement."

"Poor thing!" said the first lady, whose name was Mrs. Bell, "she'll keep no more engagements of that kind."

"Why so? Is she dead?" The tone in which these brief questions were asked, evinced no lively interest in the fate of the poor sewing-girl.

"Not dead; but very near the end of life's weary pilgrimage."

"Ah, well! we must all die, I suppose—though it's no pleasant thing to think about. But I am glad you called in this morning"—the lady's voice rose into a more cheerful tone—"I was just about putting on my things to go down to Mrs. Bobinet's opening. You intend going, of course. I shall be so delighted to have you along, for I want to consult your taste about a bonnet."

"I came out for a different purpose altogether, Mrs. Ellis," said Mrs. Bell, "and have called to ask you to go with me."

"Where?"

"To see Anna May."

"What!—that poor seamstress of whom you just spoke?" There was a look of unfeigned surprise in the lady's countenance.

"Yes; the poor seamstress, Anna May. Her days in this world are nearly numbered. I was to see her yesterday, and found her very low. She cannot long remain on this side the river of death. I am now on my way to her mother's house. Will you not go with me?"

"No, no," replied Mrs. Ellis, quickly, while a shadow fell over her face; "why should I go? I never took any particular interest in the girl. And as for dying, every thing in relation thereto is unpleasant to me. I can't bear to think of death: it makes me shudder all over."

"You have never looked in the face of death," said Mrs. Lee.

"And never wish to," replied Mrs. Ellis, feelingly. "Oh, if it wasn't for this terrible consummation, what a joyful thing life might be!"

"Anna May has looked death in the face; but does not find his aspect so appalling. She calls him a beautiful angel, who is about to take her by the hand, and lead her up gently and lovingly to her Father's house."

There came into the face of Mrs. Ellis a sudden look of wonder.

"Are you in earnest, Mrs. Bell?"

"Altogether in earnest."

"The mind of the girl is unbalanced."

"No, Mrs. Ellis; never was it more evenly poised. Come with me: it will do you good."

"Don't urge me, Mrs. Bell. If I go, it will make me sad for a week. Is the sick girl in want any comfort?—I will freely minister thereto. But I do not wish to look upon death."

"In this aspect it is beautiful to look upon. Go with me, then. The experience will be something accompany you through life. The image of frightful monster is in your mind; you may now have it displaced by the form of an angel."

"How strangely you talk, Mrs. Bell! How can death be an angel? Is any thing more terrible than death?"

"The phantom called death, which a diseased imagination conjures up, may be terrible to look upon; but death itself is a kind messenger, whose it is to summon us from this world of shadows and changes, to a world of eternal light and unfading beauty. But come, Mrs. Ellis; I must urge you to go with me. Do not fear a shock to your feelings, for none will be experienced."

So earnest were Mrs. Bell's persuasions, that her friend at last consented to go with her. At no great distance from the elegant residence of Mrs. Ellis, in an obscure neighbourhood, was a small house, humble in exterior, and modestly, yet neatly attired within. At the door of this house the ladies paused, and were admitted by a woman somewhat advanced in years, on whose mild face sorrow and holy resignation were beautifully blended.

"How is your daughter?" inquired Mrs. Bell, as soon as they were seated in the small, neat parlour.

"Not so strong as when you were here yesterday," was answered, with a faint smile. "She is sinking hourly."

"But continues in the same tranquil, heavenly state?"

"Oh yes." There was a sweet, yet touching earnestness in the mother's voice. "Dear child! Her life has been pure and unselfish; and now, when her change is about to come, all is peace, and hope, and patient waiting for the time when she will be clothed upon with immortality."

"Is she strong enough to see any one?" asked Mrs. Bell.

"The presence of others in no way disturbs her. Will you walk up into her chamber, friends?"

The two ladies ascended the narrow stairs, and Mrs. Ellis found herself, for the first time in many years, in the presence of one about to die. A slender girl, with large, mild eyes, and face almost as white as the pillow it pressed, was before her. The unmistakable signs of speedy dissolution were on the pale, shrunken features; not beautiful, in the ordinary acceptation of beauty, but from the pure spirit within. Radiant with heavenly light was the smile that instantly played upon her lips.

"How are you to-day, Anna?" kindly inquired Mrs. Bell, as she took the shadowy hand of the dying girl.

"Weaker in body than when you were here yesterday," was answered; "but stronger in spirit."

"I have brought Mrs. Ellis to see you. You remember Mrs. Ellis?"

Anna lifted her bright eyes to the face of Mrs. Ellis, and said—

"Oh yes, very well;" and she feebly extended her hand. The lady touched her hand with an emotion akin to awe. As yet, the scene oppressed and bewildered her. There was something about it that was dreamlike and unreal. "Death! death!" she questioned with herself; "can this be dying?"

"Your day will soon close, Anna," said Mrs. Bell, in a cheerful tone.

"Or, as we say," quickly replied Anna, smiling, "my morning will soon break. It is only a kind of twilight here. I am waiting for the day-dawn."

"My dear young lady," said Mrs. Ellis, with much earnestness, bending over the dying girl as she spoke—the newness and strangeness of the scene had so wrought upon her feelings, that she could not repress their utterance—"Is all indeed as you say? Are you inwardly so calm, so hopeful, so confident of the morning? Forgive me such a question, at such a moment. But the thought of death has ever been terrible to me; and now, to see a fellow-mortal standing, as you are, so near the grave, and yet speaking in cheerful tones of the last agony, fills me with wonder. Is it all real? Are you so full of heavenly tranquillity?"

Was the light dimmed in Anna's eyes by such pressing questions? Did they turn her thoughts too realizingly upon the "last agony?" Oh no! Even in the waning hours of life, her quickest impulse was to render service to another. Earnest, therefore, was her desire to remove from the lady's mind this fear of death, even though she felt the waters of Jordan already touching her own descending feet.

"God is love," she said, and with an emphasis that gave to the mind of Mrs. Ellis a new appreciation of the words. "In his love he made us, that he might bless us with infinite and eternal blessings, and these await us in heaven. And now that he sends an angel to take me by the hand and lead me up to my heavenly home, shall I tremble and fear to accompany the celestial messenger? Does the child, long separated from a loving parent, shrink at the thought of going home, or ask the hours to linger? Oh no!"

"But all is so uncertain," said Mrs. Ellis, eager to penetrate further into the mystery.

"Uncertain!" There was something of surprise in the voice of Anna May. "God is truth as well as love; and both in his love and truth he is unchangeable. When, as Divine Truth, he came to our earth, and spake as never man spake, he said, 'In my Father's house are many mansions. I go to prepare a place for you.' The heavens and the earth may pass away, Mrs. Ellis, but not a jot or tittle of the divine word can fail."

"Ah! but the preparation for those heavenly mansions!" said Mrs. Ellis. "The preparation, Anna! Who may be certain of this?"

The eyes of the sick girl closed, the long lashes resting like a dark fringe on her snowy cheek. For more than a moment she lay silent and motionless; then looking up, she answered—

"God is love. If we would be with him, we must be like him."

"How are we to be like him, Anna?" asked Mrs. Ellis.

"He is love; but not a love of himself. He loves and seeks to bless others. We must do the same."

"And have you, Anna"—

But the words died on the lips of the speaker. Again had the drooping lashes fallen, and the pale lids closed over the beautiful eyes. And now a sudden light shone through the transparent tissue of that wan face—a light, the rays of which none who saw them needed to be told were but gleams of the heavenly morning just breaking for the mortal sleeper.

How hushed the room—how motionless the group that bent forward toward the one just passing away! Was it the rustle of angels garments that penetrated the inward sense of hearing?

It is over! The pure spirit of that humble girl, who, in her sphere, was loving, and true, and faithful, hath ascended to the God in whose infinite love she reposed a childlike and unwavering confidence. Calmly and sweetly she went to sleep, like an infant on its mother's bosom, knowing that the everlasting arms were beneath and around her.

And thus, in the by-ways and obscure places of life, are daily passing away the humble, loving, true-hearted ones. The world esteems them lightly; but they are precious in the sight of God. When the time of their departure comes, they shrink not back in fear, but lift their hands trustingly to the angel messenger, whom their Father sends to lead them up to their home in heaven. With them is the true "Euthanasy."

"Is not that a new experience in life?" said Mrs. Bell, as the two ladies walked slowly homeward. With a deep sigh, the other answered—

"New and wonderful. I scarcely comprehend what I have seen. Such a lesson from such a source! How lightly I thought of that poor sewing-girl, who came and went so unobtrusively! How little dreamed I that so rich a jewel was in so plain a casket! Ah! I shall be wiser for this—wiser, and I may hope, better. Oh, to be able to die as she has died!—what of mere earthly good would I not cheerfully sacrifice!"

"It is for us all," calmly answered Mrs. Bell. "The secret we have just heard—we must be like God."

"How—how?"

"He loves others out of himself, and seeks their good. If we would be like him, we must do the same."

Yes; this is the secret of an easy death, and the only true secret.

THREE SCENES IN THE LIFE OF A WORLDLING.
SCENE FIRST.

"IT is in vain to urge me, brother Robert. Out into the world I must go. The impulse is on me. I should die of inaction here."

"You need not be inactive. There is work to do. I shall never be idle."

"And such work! Delving in and grovelling close to the very ground. And for what? Oh no, Robert. My ambition soars beyond your 'quiet cottage in a sheltered vale.' My appetite craves something more than simple herbs and water from the brook. I have set my heart on attaining wealth; and, where there is a will there is always a way."

"Contentment is better than wealth."

"A proverb for drones."

"No, William; it is a proverb for the wise."

"Be it for the wise or simple, as commonly understood, it is no proverb for me. As a poor plodder along the way of life, it were impossible for me to know content. So urge me no further, Robert. I am going out into the world a wealth-seeker, and not until wealth is gained do I purpose to return."

"What of Ellen, Robert?"

The young man turned quickly toward his brother, visibly disturbed, and fixed his eyes upon him with an earnest expression.

"I love her as my life," he said, with a strong emphasis on his words.

"Do you love wealth more than life, William?"

"Robert!"

"If you love Ellen as your life, and leave her for the sake of getting riches, then you must love money more than life."

"Don't talk to me after this fashion. I cannot bear it. I love Ellen tenderly and truly. I am going forth as well for her sake as my own. In all the good fortune that comes as the meed of effort, she will be a sharer."

"You will see her before you leave us?"

"No. I will neither pain her nor myself by a parting interview. Send her this letter and this ring."

A few hours later, and the brothers stood with tightly grasped hands, gazing into each other's faces.

"Farewell, Robert."

"Farewell, William. Think of the old homestead as still your home. Though it is mine, in the division of our patrimony, let your heart come back to it as yours. Think of it as home; and, should fortune cheat you with the apples of Sodom, return to it again. Its doors will ever be open, and its hearth-fire bright for you as of old. Farewell."

And they turned from each other, one going out into the restless world, an eager seeker for its wealth and honours; the other to linger among the pleasant places dear to him by every association of childhood, there to fill up the measure of his days—not idly, for he was no drone in the social hive.

On the evening of that day, two maidens sat alone, each in the sanctuary of her own chamber. There was a warm glow on the cheeks of one, and a glad light in her eyes. Pale was the other's face, and wet her drooping lashes. And she that sorrowed held an open letter in her hand. It was full of tender words; but the writer loved wealth more than the maiden, and had gone forth to seek the mistress of his soul. He would "come back;" but when? Ah, what a vail of uncertainty was upon the future! Poor stricken heart! The other maiden—she of the glowing cheeks and dancing eyes—held also a letter in her hand. It was from the brother of the wealth-seeker; and it was also full of loving words; and it said that, on the morrow, he would come to bear her as a bride to his pleasant home. Happy maiden!

SCENE SECOND.

TEN years have passed. And what of the wealth-seeker? Has he won the glittering prize? What of the pale-faced maiden he left in tears? Has he returned to her? Does she share now his wealth and honour? Not since the day he went forth from the home of his childhood has a word of intelligence from the wanderer been received; and, to those he left behind him, he is now as one who has passed the final bourne. Yet he still dwells among the living.

In a far-away, sunny clime, stands a stately mansion. We will not linger to describe the elegant exterior, to hold up before the reader's imagination a picture of rural beauty, exquisitely heightened by art, but enter its spacious hall, and pass up to one of its most luxurious chambers. How hushed and solemn the pervading atmosphere! The inmates, few in number, are grouped around one on whose white forehead Time's trembling finger has written the word "Death." Over her bends a manly form. There—his face is toward you. Ah! You recognise the wanderer—the wealth-seeker. What does he here? What to him is the dying one? His wife! And has he, then, forgotten the maiden whose dark lashes lay wet on her pale cheeks for many hours after she read his parting words? He has not forgotten, but been false to her. Eagerly sought he the prize, to contend for which he went forth. Years came and departed; yet still hope mocked him with ever-attractive and ever-fading illusions. To-day he stood with his hand just ready to seize the object of his wishes—to-morrow, a shadow mocked him. At last, in an evil hour, he bowed down his manhood prostrate even to the dust in mammon-worship, and took to himself a bride, rich in golden attractions, but poorer, as a woman, than even the beggar at his father's gate. What a thorn in his side she proved!—a thorn ever sharp and ever piercing. The closer he attempted to draw her to his bosom, the deeper went the points into his own, until, in the anguish of his soul, again and again he flung her passionately from him.

Five years of such a life! Oh, what is there of earthly good to compensate therefor? But, in this last desperate throw, did the worldling gain the wealth, station, and honour he coveted? He had wedded the only child of a man whose treasure might be counted by hundreds of thousands; but, in doing so, he had failed to secure the father's approval or confidence. The stern old man regarded him as a mercenary interloper, and ever treated him as such. For five years, therefore, he fretted and chafed in the narrow prison whose gilded bars his own hands had forged. How often, during that time, had his heart wandered back to the dear old home, and the beloved ones with whom he had passed his early years And ah! how many, many times came between him and the almost hated countenance of his wife, the gentle, loving face of that one to whom he had been false! How often her soft blue eyes rested on his own! How often he started and looked up suddenly, as if her sweet voice came floating on the air!

And so the years moved on, the chain galling more deeply, and a bitter sense of humiliation as well as bondage robbing him of all pleasure in life.

Thus it is with him when, after ten years, we find him waiting, in the chamber of death, for the stroke that is to break the fetters that so long have bound him. It has fallen. He is free again. In dying, the sufferer made no sign. Sullenly she plunged into the dark profound, so impenetrable to mortal eyes, and as the turbid waves closed, sighing, over her, he who had called her wife turned from the couch on which her frail body remained, with an inward "Thank God! I am a man again!"

One more bitter drug yet remained for his cup. Not a week had gone by, ere the father of his dead wife spoke to him these cutting words—

"You were nothing to me while my daughter lived—you are less than nothing now. It was my wealth, not my child, that you loved. She has passed away. What affection would have given to her, dislike will never bestow on you. Henceforth we are strangers."

When next the sun went down on that stately mansion which the wealth-seeker had coveted, he was a wanderer again—poor, humiliated, broken in spirit.

How bitter had been the mockery of all his early hopes! How terrible the punishment he had suffered!

SCENE THIRD.

ONE more eager, almost fierce struggle with alluring fortune, in which the worldling came near steeping his soul in crime, and then fruitless ambition died in his bosom.

"My brother said well," he murmured, as a ray of light fell suddenly on the darkness of his spirit: "Contentment is better than wealth. Dear brother! Dear old home! Sweet Ellen! Ah, why did I leave you? Too late! too late! A cup, full of the wine of life, was at my lips; but I turned my head away, asking for a more fiery and exciting draught. How vividly comes before me now that parting scene! I am looking into my brother's face. I feel the tight grasp of his hand. His voice is in my ears. Dear brother! And his parting words, I hear them now, even more earnestly than when they were first spoken:—'Should fortune cheat you with the apples of Sodom, return to your home again. Its doors will ever be open, and its hearth-fires bright for you as of old.' Ah! do the fires still burn? How many years have passed since I went forth! And Ellen? But I dare not think of her. It is too late—too late! Even if she be living and unchanged in her affections, I can never lay this false heart at her feet. Her look of love would smite me as with a whip of scorpions."

The step of time had fallen so lightly on the flowery path of those to whom contentment was a higher boon than wealth, that few footmarks were visible. Yet there had been changes in the old homestead. As the smiling years went by, each, as it looked in at the cottage-window, saw the home circle widening, or new beauty crowning the angel brows of happy children. No thorn in his side had Robert's gentle wife proved. As time passed on, closer and closer was she drawn to his bosom; yet never a point had pierced him. Their home was a type of paradise.

It is near the close of a summer day. The evening meal is spread, and they are about gathering around the table, when a stranger enters. His words are vague and brief, his manner singular, his air slightly mysterious. Furtive, yet eager glances go from face to face.

"Are these all your children?" he asks, surprise and admiration mingling in his tones.

"All ours. And, thank God! the little flock is yet unbroken."

The stranger averts his face. He is disturbed by emotions that it is impossible to conceal.

"Contentment is better than wealth," he murmurs. "Oh that I had earlier comprehended this truth!"

The words were not meant for others; but the utterance had been too distinct. They have reached the ears of Robert, who instantly recognises in the stranger his long wandering, long mourned brother.

"William!"

The stranger is on his feet. A moment or two the brothers stand gazing at each other, then tenderly embrace.

"William!"

How the stranger starts and trembles! He had not seen, in the quiet maiden, moving among and ministering to the children so unobtrusively, the one he had parted from years before—the one to whom he had been so false. But her voice has startled his ears with the familiar tones of yesterday.

"Ellen!" Here is an instant oblivion of all the intervening years. He has leaped back over the gloomy gulf, and stands now as he stood ere ambition and lust for gold lured him away from the side of his first and only love. It is well both for him and the faithful maiden that he can so forget the past as to take her in his arms and clasp her almost wildly to his heart. But for this, conscious shame would have betrayed his deeply repented perfidy.

And here we leave them, reader. "Contentment is better than wealth." So the wordling proved, after a bitter experience—which may you be spared! It is far better to realize a truth perceptively, and thence make it a rule of action, than to prove its verity in a life of sharp agony. But how few are able to rise into such a realization!

MATCH-MAKING.

"YOU are a sly girl, Mary."

"Not by general reputation, I believe, Mrs. Martindale."

"Oh no. Every one thinks you a little paragon of propriety. But I can see as deep as most people."

"You might as well talk in High Dutch to me, Mrs. Martindale. You would be equally intelligible."

"You are a very innocent girl, Mary."

"I hope I am. Certainly I am not conscious of wishing harm to any one. But pray, Mrs. Martindale, oblige me by coming a little nearer to the point."

"You don't remember any thing about Mrs. Allenson's party—of course?"

"It would be strange if I did not."

"Oh yes. Now you begin to comprehend a little."

"Do speak out plainly, Mrs. Martindale!"

"So innocent! Ah me, Mary! you are a sly girl. You didn't see any thing of a young man there with dark eyes and hair, and a beautiful white, high forehead?"

"If there was an individual there, answering to your description, it is highly probable that I did see him. But what then?"

"Oh, nothing, of course!"

"You are trifling with me, Mrs. Martindale."

"Seriously, then, Mary, I was very much pleased to notice the attentions shown you by Mr. Fenwick, and more pleased at seeing how much those attentions appeared to gratify you. He is a young man in a thousand."

"I am sure I saw nothing very particular in his attentions to me; and I am very certain that I was also more gratified at the attentions shown by him, than I was by those of other young men present."

"Of course not."

"You seem to doubt my word?"

"Oh no—I don't doubt your word. But on these subjects young ladies feel themselves privileged to—to"——

"To what, Mrs. Martindale?"

"Nothing—only. But don't you think Mr. Fenwick a charming young man?"

"I didn't perceive any thing very remarkable about him."

"He did about you. I saw that, clearly."

"How can you talk so to me, Mrs. Martindale?"

"Oh la! Do hear the girl! Did you never have a beau, Mary?"

"Yes, many a one. What of it?"

"And a lover too?"

"I know nothing about lovers."

As Mary Lester said this, her heart made a fluttering bound, and an emotion, new and strange, but sweet, swelled and trembled in her bosom.

"But you soon will, Mary, or I'm mistaken."

Mrs. Martindale saw the cheek of the fair girl kindle, and her eye brighten, and she said to herself, with an inward smile of satisfaction—

"I'll make a match of it yet—see if I don't! What a beautiful couple they will be!"

Mrs. Martindale was one of that singular class of elderly ladies whose chief delight consists in match-making. Many and many a couple had she brought together in her time, and she lived in the pleasing hope of seeing many more united. It was a remarkable fact, however, that in nearly every instance where her kind offices had been interposed, the result had not been the very happiest in the world. This fact, however, never seemed to strike her. The one great end of her life was to get people together—to pair them off. Whether they jogged on harmoniously together, or pulled separate ways, was no concern of hers. Her business was to make the matches. As to living in harmony, or the opposite, that concerned the couples themselves, and to that they must look themselves. It was enough for her to make the matches, without being obliged to accord the dispositions.

As in every thing else, practice makes perfect, so in this occupation, practice gave to Mrs. Martindale great skill in discerning character—at least, of such character as she could operate on. And she could, moreover, tell the progressive states of mind of those upon whom she exercised her kind offices, almost as truly as if she heard them expressed in words. It was, therefore, clear to her, after her first essay, that Mary Lester's affections might very easily be brought out and made to linger about the young man whom she had, in her wisdom, chosen as her husband. As Mary was a very sweet girl, and, moreover, had a father well to do in the world, she had no fears about interesting Mr. Fenwick in her favour.

Only a few days passed before Mrs. Martindale managed to throw herself into the company of the young man.

"How were you pleased with the party, Mr. Fenwick?" she began.

"At Mrs. Allenson's?"

"Yes."

"Very much."

"So I thought."

"Did I seem, then, particularly pleased?"

"I thought so."

"Indeed! Well, I can't say that I was interested a great deal more than I usually am on such occasions."

"Not a great deal more?"

"No, I certainly was not."

"But a little more?"

"Perhaps I was; but I cannot be positive."

"Oh yes. I know it. And I'm of the opinion that you were not the only person there who was interested a little more than usual."

"Ah, indeed! And who was the other, pray?"

"A dear little girl, whom I could mention."

"Who was she?"

"The sweetest young lady in the room."

"Well, what was her name?"

"Can't you guess?"

"I am not good at guessing."

"Try."

"Mary Lester?"

"Of course! Ha! ha! ha! I knew it."

"Knew what?"

"Oh yes, Mr. Innocence! Knew what!"

"You are disposed to be quite merry, Mrs. Martindale."

"I always feel merry when I see a young couple like you and Mary Lester mutually pleased with each other."

"Mutually pleased?"

"Of course, mutually pleased."

"How do you know that, Mrs. Martindale?"

"Haven't I got a good pair of eyes in my head?"

"Very good, I should certainly think, to make such a wonderful discovery."

"Seriously, though, Mr. Fenwick, do you not think Mary Lester a very sweet girl?"

"Certainly I do."

"And just such a one as you could love?"

"Any one, it seems to me, might love Mary Lester; but then, it is just as apparent that she could not love any one who might chance to offer."

"Of course not. And I should be very sorry to think that she could. But of one thing I am certain, she cannot look upon you with unfavourable eyes."

"Mrs. Martindale!"

"I am in earnest, Mr. Fenwick."

"What reason have you for thinking so?"

"Very good reason. I had my eyes on you both at Mrs. Allenson's party, and I saw as plain as could be that Mary was deeply interested. Since then, I have met her, and observed her eye brighten and her cheek kindle at the mention of your name. Mr. Fenwick, she is a prize well worth winning, and may be yours."

"Are you, then, really serious?" the young man now said, his tone and manner changing.

"Assuredly I am, Mr. Fenwick."

"Mary Lester, you know, moves in a circle above my own; that is, her father is accounted rich, and I am known to have nothing but my own energies to depend upon."

"All that is nothing. Win her affections, and she must be yours."

"But I am not so certain that I can do that."

"Nonsense! It is half done already."

"You seem very positive about the matter."

"Because I am never mistaken on these subjects. I can tell, the moment I see a young couple together, whether they will suit each other or not."

"And you think, then, that we will just suit?"

"Certainly I do."

"I only wish that I could think so."

"Do you, indeed? I am glad to hear you say that. I thought you could not be insensible to the charms of so sweet a girl."

"Do you, then, really believe that if I offered myself to Mary Lester, she would accept me?"

"If you went the right way about it, I am sure she would."

"What do you mean by the right way?"

"The right way for you, of course, is to endeavour to win her affections. She is already, I can see, strongly prepossessed in your favour, but is not herself aware to what extent her feelings are interested. Throw yourself into her company as much as you can, and when in her company pay her the kindest attentions. But do not visit her at her own house at present, or her father may crush the whole affair. When I see her again, I will drop a word in your favour."

"I am certainly very much indebted to you, Mrs. Martindale, for your kind hints and promised interference. I have often felt drawn toward Mary, but always checked the feeling, because I had no idea that I, could make an impression on her mind."

"Faint heart never won fair lady," was Mrs. Martindale's encouraging response.

"Well, Mary," said the lady to Miss Lester, a few days afterward, "have you seen Mr. Fenwick since?"

"Mr. Fenwick!" said she, in tones of affected surprise.

"Yes, Mr. Fenwick."

"No—of course not. Why do you ask so strange a question? He does not visit me."

"Don't he? Well, I have seen him."

"Have you? Then I hope you were very much delighted with his company, for he seems to be a favourite of yours."

"He certainly is a favourite of mine, Mary. I have known him for a good many years, and have always esteemed him highly. There are few young men who can claim to be his equal."

"I doubt not but there are hundreds to be met with every day as good as he."

"Perhaps so, Mary. I have not, however, been so fortunate as to come across them."

"No doubt he is a paragon!"

"Whether he be one or not, he at least thinks there is no one like you."

"Like me!" ejaculated Mary, taken thus suddenly by surprise, while the colour mounted to her face, and deepened about her eyes and forehead.

"Yes, like you. The fact is, Mary, he thinks and speaks of you in the kindest terms. You have evidently interested him very much."

"I certainly never intended to do so, Mrs. Martindale."

"Of course not, Mary. I never supposed for a moment that you had. Still he is interested, and deeply so."

Having ventured thus far, Mrs. Martindale deemed it prudent to say no more for the present, but to leave her insinuations to work upon Mary's heart what they were designed to effect. She was satisfied that all was as she could wish —that both Fenwick and Mary were interested in each other; and she knew enough of the human heart, and of her own power over it, when exercised in a certain way, to know that it would not be long before they were much more deeply interested.

Like all the rest of Mrs. Martindale's selections of parties for matrimony, the present was a very injudicious one. Mary was only seventeen—too young, by three or four years, to be able properly to judge of character; and Fenwick was by no means a suitable man for her husband. He was himself only about twenty-one, with a character not yet fully decided, though the different constituents of his mind were just ready to take their various positions, and fixed and distinctive forms. Unfortunately, these mental and moral relations were not truly balanced; there was an evident bias of selfishness and evil over generous and true principles. As Mrs. Martindale was no profound judge of character, she could not, of course, make a true discrimination of Fenwick's moral fitness for the husband of Mary Lester. Indeed, she never attempted to analyze character, nor had she an idea of any thing beneath the surface. Personal appearance, an affable exterior, and a little flattery of herself, were the three things which, in her estimation, went to make up a perfect character —were enough to constitute the beau ideal of a husband for any one.

Mary's father was a merchant of considerable wealth and standing in society, and possessing high-toned feelings and principles. Mary was his oldest child. He loved her tenderly, and, moreover, felt all a parent's pride in one so young, so lovely, and so innocent.

Fenwick had, until within a few months, been a clerk in a retail dry-goods store, at a very small salary. A calculating, but not too honest a wholesale dealer in the same line, desirous of getting rid of a large stock of unsaleable goods, proposed to the young man to set him up in business—a proposition which was instantly accepted. The credit thus furnished to Fenwick was an inducement for others to sell to him; and so, without a single dollar of capital, he obtained a store full of goods. The scheme of the individual who had thus induced him to venture upon a troubled and uncertain sea, was to get paid fair prices for his own depreciated goods out of Fenwick's first sales, and then gradually to withdraw his support, compelling him to buy of other jobbing houses, until his indebtedness to him would be but nominal. He was very well assured that the young merchant could not stand it over a year or two, and for that length of time only by a system of borrowing and accommodations; but as to the result he cared nothing, so that he effected a good sale of a bad stock.

Notwithstanding such an unpromising condition of his affairs, even if fully known to Mr. Lester, that gentleman would not have strongly opposed a union of his daughter with Mr. Fenwick, had he been a man of strong mind, intelligence, energy, and high-toned principles—for he was philosopher enough to know that these will elevate a man under any circumstances. But Fenwick had no decided points in his character. He had limited intelligence, and no energy arising from clear perceptions and strong resolutions. He was a man fit to captivate a young and innocent girl, but not to hold the affection of a generous-minded woman.

In the natural order of events, such a circumstance as a marriage union between the daughter of Mr. Lester, and an individual like Fenwick, was not at all likely to occur. But a meddlesome woman, who, by the accident of circumstances, had found free access to the family of Mr. Lester, set herself seriously at work to interfere with the orderly course of things, and effect a conjunction between two in no way fitted for each other, either in external circumstances or similarity of character. But let us trace the progress of this artificial passion, fanned into a blaze by the officious Mrs. Martindale. After having agitated the heart of Mary with the idea of being beloved, while she coolly calculated its effects upon her, the match-monger sought an early opportunity for another interview with Fenwick.

"I have seen Mary since we last met," she said.

"Well, do you think I have any thing to hope?"

"Certainly I do. I mentioned your name to her on purpose, and I could see that the heart of the dear little thing began to flutter at the very sound; and when I bantered her, she blushed, and was all confusion."

"When shall I be able to meet her again?"

"Next week, I think. There is to be a party at Mrs. Cameron's and as I am a particular friend of the family, I will endeavour to get you an invitation."

"Mary is to be there, of course?"

"Certainly."

"Are you sure that you can get me invited?"

"Yes, I think so. Mrs. Cameron, it is true, has some exclusive notions of her own; but I have no doubt of being able to remove them."

"Try, by all means."

"You may depend on me for that," was Mrs. Martindale's encouraging reply.

The evening of Mrs. Cameron's party soon came around. Mrs. Martindale had been as good as her word, and managed to get Fenwick invited, although he had never in his life met either Mr. or Mrs. Cameron. But he had no delicate and manly scruples on the subject. All he desired was to get invited; the way in which it was done was of no consequence to him.

Mary Lester was seated by the side of her interested friend when the young man entered. Her heart gave a quick bound as she saw him come in, while a pleasant thrill pervaded her bosom. He at once advanced toward them, while Mrs. Martindale rose, and after receiving him with her blandest manner, presented him to Mary, so as to give him an opportunity for being in her society at once. Both were, as might very naturally be supposed, a good deal embarrassed, for each was conscious that now a new relation existed between them. This their very kind friend observed, and with much tact introduced subjects of conversation, until she had paved the way, for a freer intercourse, and then she left them alone for a brief period, not, however, without carefully observing them, to see how they "got along together," as she mentally expressed it.

She had little cause for further concern on this account, for Fenwick had a smooth and ready tongue in his head, and five years behind the counter of a retail dealer had taught him how to use it. Instead of finding it necessary to prompt them, the wily Mrs. Martindale soon discovered that her kind offices were needed to restrain them a little, lest the evidence of their being too well pleased with each other should be discovered by the company.

Two or three interviews more were all that were needed to bring about a declaration from the young man. Previous to his taking this step, however, Mrs. Martindale had fully prepared Mary's mind for it.

"You own to me, Mary," said she, during one of the many conversations now held with her on the subject of Fenwick's attentions, "that you love him?"

"I do, Mrs. Martindale," the young lady replied, in a tone half sad, leaning at the same time upon the shoulder of her friend. "But I am conscious that I have been wrong in permitting my affections to become so much interested without having consulted my mother."

"It will never do for you to consult her now, Mary, for she does not know Mr. Fenwick as you and I know him. She will judge of him, as will your father, from appearances, and forbid you to keep his company."

"I am sure that such will be the case, and you cannot tell how it troubles me. From childhood up I have been taught to confide in them, and, except in this thing, have never once deceived them. The idea of doing so now, is one that gives me constant pain. I feel that I have not acted wisely in this matter."

"Nonsense, Mary! Parents never think with their children in these matters. It would make no odds whom you happened to love, they would most certainly oppose you. I never yet knew a young lady whose parents fully approved her choice of a husband."

"I feel very certain that mine will not approve my choice; and I cannot bear the idea of their displeasure. Sometimes I feel half determined to tell them all, let the consequences be what they may."

"Oh no, no, Mary! not for the world. They would no doubt take steps to prevent your again meeting each other."

"What, then, shall I do, Mrs. Martindale?"

"See Mr. Fenwick whenever an opportunity offers, and leave the rest to me. I will advise you when and how to act."

The almost involuntary admissions made by Mary in this conversation, were at once conveyed to the ears of Fenwick, who soon sought an opportunity openly to declare his love. Of course, his suit was not rejected. Thus, under the advice and direction of a most injudicious woman, who had betrayed the confidence placed in her, was a young girl, unacquainted with life, innocent and unsuspicious, wooed and won, and her parents wholly ignorant of the circumstance.

Thoughts of marriage follow quickly a declaration of love. Once with the prize in view, Fenwick was eager to have it wholly in his possession. Mrs. Martindale was, of course, the mutual friend and adviser, and she urged an immediate clandestine marriage. For many weeks Mary resisted the persuasions of both. Fenwick and Mrs. Martindale; but at last, in a state of half distraction of mind, she consented to secretly leave her father's house, and throw herself upon the protection of one she had not known for six months, and of whose true character she had no certain knowledge.

"Mary is out a great deal of late, it seems to me," Mr. Lester remarked, as he sat alone with his wife one evening about ten o'clock.

"So I was just thinking. There is, scarcely an evening now in the week that she has not an engagement somewhere."

"I cannot say that I much approve of such a course myself. There is always danger of a girl, just at Mary's age, forming injudicious preferences for young men, if she be thrown much into their company, unattended by a proper adviser."

"Mrs. Martindale is very fond of Mary, and I believe is with her a good deal."

"Mrs. Martindale? Humph! Do you know that I have no great confidence in that woman?"

"Why?"

"Have you forgotten the hand she had in bringing about that most unfortunate marriage of Caroline Howell?"

"I had almost forgotten it. Or, rather, I never paid much attention to the rumour in regard to her interference in the matter; because, you know, people will talk."

"And to some purpose, often; at least, I am persuaded that there is truth in all that is alleged in this instance. And now that my thoughts begin to run in this way, I do really feel concerned lest the reason of Mary's frequent absence of late, in company with Mrs. Martindale, has some reference to a matter of this kind. Have you not observed some change in her of late?"

"She has not been very cheerful for the last two or three months."

"So I have once or twice thought, but supposed it was only my imagination. If this, then, be true, it is our duty to be on our guard—to watch over Mary with a careful eye, and to know particularly into what company she goes."

"I certainly agree with you that we ought to do so. Heaven grant that our watchfulness do not come too late!" Mrs. Lester said, a sudden feeling of alarm springing up in her bosom.

"It is a late hour for her to be from home, and we not apprized of where she is," the father remarked anxiously.

"It is, indeed. She has rarely stayed out later than nine o'clock."

"Who has been in the habit of coming home with her?"

"Usually Mrs. Martindale has accompanied her home, and this fact has thrown me off my guard."

"It should have put you on your guard; for a woman like Mrs. Martindale, gossiping about as she does, night after night, with young folks, cannot, it seems to me, have the best ends in view."

"She seems to be a very well-disposed woman."

"That is true. And yet I have been several times persuaded that she was one of the detestable tribe of match-makers."

"Surely not."

"I am afraid that it is too true. And if it be so, Mary is in dangerous company."

"Indeed she is. From this time forth we must guard her more carefully. Of all things in the world, I dread an improper marriage for Mary. If she should throw away her affections upon an unworthy object, how sad would be her condition! Her gentle spirit, wounded in the tenderest part, would fail, and droop, and pine away in hopeless sorrow. Some women have a strength of character that enables them to rise superior, in a degree, to even such an affliction; but Mary could not bear it."

"I feel deeply the truth of what you say," replied Mr. Lester. "Her affections are ardent, and easily called out. We have been to blame in not thinking more seriously of this matter before."

"I wish she would come home! It is growing far too late for her to be absent," the mother said, in a voice of anxious concern.

Then succeeded a long and troubled silence, which continued until the clock struck eleven.

"Bless me! where can she be?" ejaculated Mr. Lester, rising and beginning to pace the floor with hurried steps.

This he continued to do for nearly a quarter of an hour, when he paused, and said—

"Do you know where Mrs. Martindale lives?"

"At No.—Pearl street."

"No doubt she can tell where Mary is."

"I think it more than probable."

"Then I will see her at once."

"Had you not better wait a little longer? I should be sorry to attract attention, or cause remark about the matter, which would be the result, if it got out that you went in search of her after eleven o'clock at night."

This had the effect to cause Mr. Lester to wait little longer. But when the clock struck twelve, he could restrain himself no further. Taking up his hat, he hurried off in the direction of Mrs. Martindale's.

"Is Mrs. Martindale at home?" he asked of the servant, who, after he had rung three or four times, found her way to the door.

"No, sir," was the reply.

"Where is she?"

"I do not know, sir."

"Will she be here to-night?"

"No, sir."

"Is she in the habit of staying away at night?"

"No, sir."

"Where did she go early in the evening?"

"I do not know, sir."

Disappointed, and doubly alarmed, Mr. Lester turned away, and retraced his steps homeward.

"Did you see her?" eagerly inquired his wife, as he entered.

"She is not at home."

"Where is she?"

"The stupid servant could not or would not tell."

"Indeed, indeed, I do not like the appearance of all this," said Mrs. Lester, with a troubled countenance.

"Nor do I. I am sadly afraid all is not right in regard to Mary."

"But she certainly could not be induced to go away with any one—in a word, to marry clandestinely."

"I should hope not. But one so innocent and unsuspecting as Mary—one with so much natural goodness of character—is most easily led away by the specious and designing, who can easily obscure their minds, and take from them their own freedom of action. For this reason, we should have guarded her much more carefully than we have done."

For two hours longer did the anxious parents wait and watch for Mary's return, but in vain. They then retired to take a brief but troubled repose.

Early on the next morning, in going into Mary's room, her mother found a letter for her, partly concealed among the leaves of a favourite volume that lay upon her table. It contained the information that she was about to marry Mr. Fenwick, and gave Mrs. Martindale as authority for the excellence of his character: The letter was written on the previous day, and the marriage was to take place that night.

With a stifled cry of anguish, Mrs. Lester sprang down the stairs, on comprehending the tenor of the letter, and, placing it in the hands of her husband, burst into tears. He read it through without visible emotion; but the intelligence fell like a dead, oppressive weight upon his heart—almost checking respiration. Slowly he seated himself upon a chair, while his head sank upon his bosom, and thus he remained almost motionless for nearly half an hour, while his wife wept and sobbed by his side.

"Mary," he at last said, in a mournful tone—"she is our child yet."

"Wretched—wretched girl!" responded Mrs. Lester; "how could she so fatally deceive herself and us?"

"Fatally, indeed, has she done so! But upon her own head will the deepest sorrow rest. I only wish that we were altogether guiltless of this sacrifice."

"But may it not turn out that this Mr. Fenwick will not prove so unworthy of her as we fear?—that he will do all in his power to make her happy?"

"Altogether a vain hope, Mary. He is evidently not a man of principle, for no man of principle would have thus clandestinely stolen away our child—which he could only have done by first perverting or blinding her natural perceptions of right. Can such an one make any pure-minded, unselfish woman happy? No!—the hope is altogether vain. He must have been conscious of his unworthiness, or he would have come forward like a man and asked for her."

Mr. and Mrs. Lester loved their daughter too well to cast her off. They at once brought her, with her husband, back to her home again, and endeavoured to make that home as pleasant to her as ever. But, alas! few months had passed away, before the scales fell from her eyes—before she perceived that the man upon whom she had lavished the wealth of her young heart's affections, could not make her happy. A weak and vain young man, Fenwick could not stand the honour of being Mr. Lester's son-in-law, without having his brain turned. He became at once an individual of great consequence—assumed airs, and played the fool so thoroughly, as not only to disgust her friends and family, but even Mary herself. His business was far too limited for a man of his importance. He desired to relinquish the retail line, and get into the jobbing trade. He stated his plans to Mr. Lester, and boldly asked for a capital of twenty thousand dollars to begin with. This was of course refused. That gentleman thought it wisdom to support him in idleness, if it came to that, rather than risk the loss of a single dollar in a business in which there was a moral certainty of failure.

Disgusted with his father-in-law's narrow-mindedness, as he called it, Fenwick attempted to make the desired change on the strength of his own credit. This scheme likewise proved a failure. And that was not all, as in the course of a twelve-month his creditors wound him up, and he came out a bankrupt.

Mr. Lester then offered him a situation as clerk in his own store; but Fenwick was a young man of too much consequence to be clerk to any man. If he could not be in business himself, he, would do no business at all, he said. That he was determined on. He could do business as well as any one, and had as much right to be in business as any one.

The consequence was, that idle habits took him into idle company, and idle company led him on to dissipation. Three years after his marriage with Mary Lester, he was a drunkard and a gambler, and she a drooping, almost heart-broken young wife and mother.

One night, nearly four years from the date of her unhappy marriage, Mary sat alone in her chamber, by the side of the bed upon which slept sweetly and peacefully a little girl nearly three years of age, the miniature image of herself. Her face was very thin and pale, and there was a wildness in her restless eyes, that betokened a troubled spirit. The time had worn on until nearly one o'clock, and still she made no movement to retire; but seemed waiting for some one, and yet not in anxious expectation. At last the door below was opened, and footsteps came shuffling along the hall, and noisily up the stairs. In a moment or two, her room-door was swung widely open, and her husband staggered in, so drunk that he could scarcely keep his feet.

"And pray what are you doing up at this time of night, ha?" said he, in drunken anger.

"You did not like it, you know, because I was in bed last night, and so I have sat up for you this time," his wife replied, soothingly.

"Well, you've no business to be up this late, let me tell you, madam. And I'm not agoing to have it. So bundle off to bed with you, in less than no time!"

"O Henry! how can you talk so to me?" poor Mary said, bursting into tears.

"You needn't go to blubbering in that way, I can tell you, madam; so just shut up! I won't have it! And see here: I must have three hundred dollars out of that stingy old father of yours to-morrow, and you must get it for me. If you don't, why, just look out for squalls."

As he said this, he threw himself heavily upon the bed, and came with his whole weight upon the body of his child. Mrs. Fenwick screamed out, sprang to the bedside, and endeavoured to drag him off the little girl. Not understanding what she meant, he rose up quickly, and threw her from him with such force, as to dash her against the wall opposite, when she fell senseless upon the floor. Just at this moment, her father, who had overheard his first angry words, burst into the room, and with the energy of suddenly aroused indignation, seized Fenwick by the collar, dragged him down-stairs, and thence threw him into the street from his hall-door, which he closed and locked after him—vowing, as he did so, that the wretch should never again cross his threshold.

All night long did poor Mrs. Fenwick lie, her senses locked in insensibility; and all through the next day she remained in the same state, in spite of every effort to restore her. Her husband several times attempted to gain admittance, but was resolutely refused.

"He never crosses my door-stone again!" the old man said; and to that resolution he determined to adhere.

Another night and another day passed, and still another night, and yet the heart-stricken young wife showed no signs of returning consciousness. It was toward evening on the fourth day, that the family, with Mrs. Martindale, who had called in, were gathered round her bed, in a state of painful and gloomy anxiety, waiting for, yet almost despairing again to see her restored to consciousness. All at once she opened her eyes, and looked up calmly into the faces of those who surrounded her bed.

"Where is little Mary?" she at length asked.

The child was instantly brought to her.

"Does Mary love mother?" she asked of the child, in a tone of peculiar tenderness.

The child drew its little arms about her neck, and kissed her pale lips and cheeks fondly.

"Yes, Mary loves mother. But mother is going away to leave Mary. Will she be a good girl?"

The little thing murmured assent, as it clung closer to its mother's bosom.

Mrs. Fenwick then looked up into the faces of her father and mother with a sad but tender smile, and said—

"You will be good to little Mary when I am gone?

"Don't talk so, Mary!—don't, my child! You are not going to leave us," her mother sobbed, while the tears fell from her eyes like rain.

"Oh no, dear! you will not leave us," said her father, in a trembling voice.

"Yes, dear mother! dear father! I must go. But you will not let any one take little Mary from you?"

"Oh no—ever! She is ours, and no one shall ever take her away."

Mrs. Fenwick then closed her eyes, while a placid expression settled upon her sweet but careworn face. Again she looked up, but with a more serious countenance. As she did so, her eyes rested upon Mrs. Martindale.

"I am about to die, Mrs. Martindale," she said, hit a calm but feeble voice —"and with my dying breath I charge upon you the ruin of my hopes and happiness. If my little girl should live to woman's estate," she added, turning to her parents, "guard her from the influence of this woman, as you would from the fangs of a serpent."

Then closing her eyes again, she sank away into a sleep that proved the sleep of death. Alas! how many like her have gone down to an early grave, or still pine on in hopeless sorrow, the victims of that miserable interference in society, which is constantly bringing young people together, and endeavouring to induce them to love and marry each other, without there being between them any true congeniality or fitness for such a relation! Of all assumed social offices, that of the match-maker is one of the most pernicious, and her character one of the most detestable. She should be shunned with the same shrinking aversion with which we shun a serpent which crosses our path.

THE RETURN; OR, WHO IS IT?

"IT'S nearly a year now since I was home," said Lucy Gray to her husband; "and so you must let me go for a few weeks."

They had been married some four or five years, and never during that time had been separated for a single night.

"I thought you called this your home," said Gray, looking up with a mock-serious air.

"I mean my old home," replied Lucy, in a half-affected tone of anger. "Or, to make it plain, I want to go, and see father and mother."

"Can't you wait three or four months, until I can go with you?" asked the young husband.

"I want to go now. You said all along that I should go in May."

"I know I did. But then I supposed that I would be able to go with you."

"Well, why can't you? I am sure you might, if you would."

"No, Lucy, I cannot possibly leave home now. But if you are very anxious to see the old folks, I can put you in the stage, and you will go safely enough. Ellen and I can take care of little Lucy, no doubt. How long a time do you wish to spend with them?"

"About three weeks or so?"

"Very well, Lucy, if you are not afraid to go lone, I have not a word to say."

"I'm not afraid, dear," replied the wife in a voice hanged and softened in its expression. "But are you perfectly willing to let me go, Henry?"

"Oh, certainly," was answered, although the tone in which the words were uttered had in it something of reluctance. "It would be selfish in me to say no. Your father and mother will be delighted receive a visit just now."

"And you think that you and Ellen can get along with little Lucy?"

"Oh yes, very well."

"I should like to go so much."

"Go, then, by all means."

"But won't you be very lonesome without me?" suggested Lucy, in whose own bosom a feeling of loneliness was already beginning to be felt at the bare idea of a separation from her husband.

"I can stand it as long as you," was Gray's laughing reply to this. "And then I shall have our dear little Lucy."

Mrs. Gray laughed in return, but did not feel as happy at the idea of "going home" as she thought she would be before her husband's consent was gained. The desire to go, however, remaining strong, it was finally settled that the visit should take place. So all the preparations were made, and in the course of a week Henry Gray saw his wife take her seat in the stage, with a feeling of regret at parting which it required all his efforts to conceal. As for Lucy, when the time came, she regretted ever having thought of going without her husband and child; but she was ashamed to let her real feelings be known. So she kept on a show of indifference, all the while that her heart was fluttering. The "good-bye" finally said, the driver cracked his whip, and off rolled the stage. Gray turned homeward with a dull, lonely feeling, and Lucy drew her vail over her face to conceal the unbidden tears from her fellow-passengers.

That night, poor Mr. Gray slept but little. How could he? His Lucy was absent, and for the first time, from his side. On the next morning, as he could think of nothing but his wife, he sat down and wrote to her, telling her how lost and lonely he felt, and how much little Lucy missed her, but still to try and enjoy herself, and by all means to write him a letter by return mail.

As for Mrs. Gray, during her journey of two whole days, she cried fully half the time, and when she got "home" at last, that is, at her father's, she looked the picture of distress, rather than the daughter full of joy at meeting her parents.

Right glad were the old people to see their dear child, but grieved at the same time, and a little hurt too, at her weakness and evident regret at having left her husband, to make them a brief visit. The real pleasure that Lucy felt at once more seeing the faces of her parents, whom she tenderly loved, was not strong enough to subdue and keep in concealment, except for a very short period at a time, her yearning desire again to be with her husband, for whom she never before experienced a feeling of such deep and earnest affection. Several times during the first day of her visit, did her mother find, her in tears, which she would quickly dash aside, and then endeavour to smile and seem cheerful.

The day after her arrival brought her a letter—the first she had ever received from her husband. How precious was every word! How often and often did she read it over, until every line was engraven on her memory! Then she sat down, and spent some two or three hours in replying to it. As she sealed this first epistle to her husband, full of tender expressions, she sighed as the wish arose in her mind, involuntarily, to go with it on its journey to the village of ——.

Long were the hours, and wearily passed, to Henry Gray. It was the sixth day of trial, before Lucy's answer came. How dear to his heart was every word of her affectionate epistle! Like her, he went over it so often, that every sentiment was fixed in his mind.

"Two weeks longer! How can I bear it?" said he, rising up, and pacing the floor backward and forward, after reading her letter for the tenth time.

On the next day, the seventh of his lonely state, Mr. Gray sat down to write again to Lucy. Several times he wrote the words, as he proceeded in the letter —"Come home soon,"—but often obliterated them. He did not wish to appear over anxious for her return, on her father and mother's account, who were much attached to her. But forgetting this reason for not urging her early return, he had commenced again writing the words, "Come home soon," when a pair of soft hands were suddenly placed over his eyes, by some one who had stolen softly up behind him.

"Guess my name," said a voice, in feigned tones.

But he had no need to guess, for a sudden cry of joy from a little toddling thing, told that "Mamma" had come.

How "Mamma" was hugged and kissed all round, need not here be told. That scene was well enough in its place, but would lose its interest in telling. It may be imagined, however, without suffering any particular detriment, by all who have a fancy for such things.

"And father, too!" suddenly exclaimed Mr. Gray, after he had almost smothered his wife with kisses, looking up with an expression of pleasure and surprise, at an old man, who stood looking on with his good-humoured face covered with smiles.

"Yes. I had to bring the good-for-nothing jade home," replied the old man advancing, and grasping his son-in-law's hand, with a hearty grip. "She did nothing but mope and cry all the while; and I don't care if she never comes to see us again, unless she brings you along to keep her in good humour."

"And I never intend going alone again," said Mrs. Gray, holding a little chubby girl to her bosom, while she kissed it over and over again, at the same time that he pressed close up to her husband's side.

The old man understood it all. He was not jealous of Lucy's affection, for he knew that she loved him as tenderly as ever. He was too glad to know that she was happy with a husband to whom she was as the apple of his eye. In about three months Lucy made another visit "home." But husband and child were along this time, and the visit proved a happy one all around. Of course "father and mother" had their jest, and their laugh, and their affectation of jealousy and anger at Lucy for her "childishness," as they termed it, when home in May; but Lucy, though half vexed at herself for what she called her weakness, nevertheless persevered in saying that she never meant to go any where again without Henry. "That was settled."

Milton Keynes UK
Ingram Content Group UK Ltd.
UKHW050645290424
441924UK00013B/700

The title "Finger Posts on the Way of Life" suggests that the stories within the book act as signposts or guides, pointing readers towards the right path in life. Arthur's writing typically focuses on moral dilemmas, ethical choices, and the consequences of one's actions.

Each story in the book likely presents a moral lesson or insight, often drawn from everyday life situations that readers could easily relate to. Arthur's writing style tends to be didactic, aiming to instruct and uplift his audience.

ISBN 978-1-83591-688-9
90000
9 781835 916889